CAN'T BUY ME FADED LOVE

CAN'T BUY ME
FADED LOVE

Stories by
Josh Rountree

With an Introduction by
Howard Waldrop

Wheatland Press
http://www.wheatlandpress.com

Wheatland Press

http://www.wheatlandpress.com

Library of Congress Cataloging-in-Publication data is available upon request.
ISBN 978-0-9794054-2-6
Printed in the United States of America
Interior design by Deborah Layne.
Cover art and design by Darin Bradley.

For Kristin.

I still want to hold your hand.

Contents

Let's Kill Him Now!
By Howard Waldrop

Josh Rountree's writing came down on me like the Assyrian on the fold.

ख

Here's how it happens with *most* new writers: somebody mentions a story they read in a magazine or anthology, and they put a name on it. A couple of months later, the name comes up again. Then you go to an SF convention and THEY'RE THE GUEST OF HONOR AND EVERYBODY (except you) HAS READ EVERY WORD THEY'RE EVER WRITTEN, THEN THEY WIN THE NEBULA, HUGO AND WORLD FANTASY AWARD all in the same year. Then, they're not a NEW WRITER ANYMORE. (In the old days, I was on the NEW WRITERS panel every convention I went to until 10 years into my so-called career…)

I'd never heard of Josh Rountree til I read this book.

ख

What a revelation: He's writing the kinds of stories me, Steven Utley, Lisa Tuttle and Joe Pumilia were *trying* to write when we were starting out.

All of us would have had heart attacks if we'd have been offered a collection so early in our careers (or, had enough *good* stories to fill one up).

Rountree is having the stories and careers we *wished for* way back then.

Everybody's been trying to do an SF/Fantasy rock'n'roll anthology for at least thirty years now. (Charles Shaar Murray said something like: "I often thought of editing an SF rock and roll anthology. Then I realized half the stories would be from the Bruce Sterling-edited MIRRORSHADES and the other half would be by Howard Waldrop.") He could now add "with four or five more by Josh Rountree."

Rountree has eliminated the middleman by doing *almost* a whole book of SF/Fantasy rock and roll stories himself. (More than *me*; more than *anybody ever* has.)

Even the Afterwords to his stories are called Liner Notes (Something I was going to have when a story of minewas to be published in a limited edition in a CD box with a Rhino™ doo-wop collection included) — see what I *mean* about my career coming true in Rountree? He also has a recommended listening list of CDs for each story; references to the stuff the story's about, or its ambiance, etc. He's usually dead right-on. He knows his stuff.

But rock and roll is *not all* he writes about, though it's never very far away. In "Nikola and the Wolf" he has a story that continues SF's fascination with the scientist that got the ticket to Palookaville (actually, Colorado Springs), Nikola Tesla. This one has a setting that gives a whole new meaning to the phrase "pirate radio."

And is he afraid to go where giants have trod? *Hell no.* Take Lester Bangs, everybody's favorite rock critic, *especially since* his death in 1982. Bruce Sterling wrote a great story, "Dorie Bangs" about *what might have been.* ("Bruce, Bruce," I said when he wrote it, "You've fucked up for the first time in your career. You've given us *people we actually care about!*") Check out Rountree's "The Review Lester Bangs Would Have Written For the New Stones Album If He'd Lived Long Enough to Witness the Fall of Humanity and the Rise of the Other" (a Lester Bangs title if ever there was one) — in which in the course of a typical L.B. rant/review we begin to see Things Have Changed.

In fact, Things Are (or Have) Changed/Changing in several of these stories.

This guy is getting a story collection just a few years into his career. I waited 17 years for my first one; other friends of mine went 20 to 30 years or more for theirs. That means: (a) the right publisher's weren't around, (b) the ones that *were* were asleep, or (c) this guy's done a solid body of work right out of the chute.

I suspect (c).

His take on rock and roll isn't mine (his p.o.v. isn't mine either — I suspect it's a couple of feet higher and a little back and to the left of mine — or anybody else's). It's solely and exclusively his own.

Say the name. Josh Rountree. Came out of nowhere. Claimjumped and backshot my mind. Ran away laughing, doing the same to anybody in sight.

The future's in good hands.

I hate hate hate hate *hate_* the bastard.

Austin, Texas
January, 2008

Can't Buy Me Faded Love

Excerpt from The New York Times, *December 9, 1980*

...Lennon was returning home from a recording session when he was shot five times in the shoulder and chest in front of his Central Park West apartment. Alleged gunman, Mark David Chapman, when asked if he knew what he'd done, reportedly replied, "I just shot John Lennon." Chapman made no effort to avoid arrest, but instead sat on the sidewalk reading a book until the police arrived.

Fans and admirers continue to flock to the site of yesterday's shooting, many erecting makeshift monuments and singing "All You Need is Love," one of the last songs Lennon recorded with his former band, The Quarrymen, before breaking ties with longtime collaborator Bob Wills. Janet Lumley, who was in attendance when the Quarrymen made their now famous appearance at Shea Stadium, flew in from Boston to pay her respects.

"This is horrible. That he could be murdered like that. How are you supposed to deal with something like this? The world has lost the greatest country songwriter of the past thirty years."

ଓ

Excerpt from Can't Buy Me Faded Love—The Unauthorized Legend of The Quarrymen, *Ernest and Shultz, 1989*

There can be little doubt that the most important pairing of musicians in the twentieth century occurred in Austin, Texas on a hot July evening in 1961. Having traveled to America less than six months earlier from his home in Liverpool, England, a young man with "too-long" hair and a slick new Telecaster reached out and seized his destiny.

"I heard about the Playboys going on tour that summer and I had to be there," said Lennon in a 1978 interview with biographer, Lon Haines. "Much of Bob's original success came before I was born, but I was a fan. More than a fan, really. That music was my life when I was a kid. My aunt used to play those 78's all the time, all the old Western Swing bands, but especially the Playboys. I never knew my father, but I remember listening to those songs and wondering if he might have gone to America to become a singer. Maybe Bob Wills was my dad, you know? I was a kid then. I reckoned Bob was the singer since the band was named after him. Later on I understood that it was his fiddle playing that really inspired me. It made me sad. It made me long for something. A father, maybe, but something else too. I wanted to be in America, and I wanted to make that kind of music."

Lennon quit his job in the Liverpool shipyards and informed his then band mates that he was leaving for the United States as soon as he could book passage on a ship.

"Don't remember where the name came from," said Lennon, "but we called our band The Beatles. We played some swing, some skiffle, and that was popular at the time, but mostly we played rock and roll. It was the hot thing and all the lads, especially Paul and Stu, were big Elvis and Little Richard fans. I liked the music too, but I reckoned it was a fad. Swing was king, and it was primed for a comeback. Needless to say, we didn't see eye to eye. I invited them all to come along with me, but they took it as a personal slight that I would consider leaving. I was gone a week later, and I never heard from any of them again."

Bob Wills recounted that first meeting with the twenty-one year old Lennon in a 1972 interview with *Life* magazine. "He was the scrawniest thing I ever saw. Looked like he hadn't eaten in a week. He'd been following us from town to town, hanging out at the shows with his guitar, always sitting right at the edge of the dance floor. Staring like he was studying up on us or something. The only reason I noticed him was that long hair of his. That was before it caught on, of course. He was crazy as a loon for going around wearing long hair and a leather jacket in the type of bars we was playing. But he didn't know no better.

"So that night in Austin, he gets there while the boys are setting up and begs me to let him sit in on a few songs. Tells me he came all the way from England to join my band. I laughed and thanked him for being such a fan, but there wasn't no way I'd let a stranger up on stage with us. Then he pulls out that blonde Telecaster of his—and I guarantee by the look of him he must have bought that damn thing with the last pennies in his pocket—and he starts them fingers dancing on the strings. Aw, lord! You know what that sounded like. I never heard anyone play like John, before or since.

"Still, I didn't invite him on stage until near the end of the set. I'm not sure why I even did it, but I did. I still remember the look in that kid's eyes when he stepped up there in his pointy shoes and beat up jeans. Everyone loves him now, but I'll testify the people in that bar didn't know what to make of a longhair taking the stage with us. Until he plugged in that guitar and we kicked into 'Take Me Back to Tulsa' He changed a lot of minds that night. Mine included."

ରଃ

Postcard from Bob Wills to Al Stricklin, July 13, 1962

Al,

Howdy from Austin! We still plan on being there the twenty-first. Always love coming back to Fort Worth. I'm bringing this kid with me that plays guitar like nobody you ever seen. He's a character, come all the way over from England. Wait till you hear him!

See you soon,
Bob

ରଃ

Excerpt from an interview with Al Stricklin, Honky Tonk Keys, December, 1979

"I was back running a Saturday night country broadcast then, this time for WBAP, and it suited me fine. I remembered my days touring with Bob fondly, but being on the road all the time takes it out of you. I was glad to have Bob back in the studio, though, and interested to hear this new guitar prodigy he'd been bragging on.

"First time I saw John he was wearing a new felt cowboy hat. Trying to be like Bob, I guess. But he looked out of place. The kid had more rock and roll in him than he cared to admit. He was a humble guy, helped everyone set up for the show, even helped set up the drums.

"We went live and I chatted on-air with Bob a bit, then the band kicked in with the Texas Playboy Theme. When John's solo came up, my jaw hit the ground. Bob was right, the kid could play. I was sitting in with the band for old time's sake, and I swear that kid playing like that inspired me. I pounded the keys that night like I hadn't in years. I ain't lying when I tell you right then I knew John Lennon was something special. Bob knew it too. You could see it in his eyes."

È

Letter from John Lennon to his Aunt Mimi

15 August, 1962

Auntie,

I'm in Texas! Sorry it's been a while since I wrote, but I think you'll be proud of me. I know how you are about the music of Mr. Bob Wills and so it might surprise you to learn I've been playing guitar in his band! Last month we played on Mr. Al Stricklin's country radio programme and he even let me play some of my songs for him. Remember "Love Me Do?" You said you liked that one. Well, so did Mr. Stricklin, and he suggested to Mr. Wills that he record it. Mr. Wills has agreed to cut a 45. If it sells, he says maybe we can do some more. Wouldn't that be fab?

With love from me to you,

John

cs

Capital Records Press Release, September 29, 1962

Straight from the Heart of Texas comes the debut LP from The Quarrymen, the hopping new band led by Western Swing legend Bob Wills. Building on the success of their hit single, "Love Me Do," the *Meet The Quarrymen* LP features the future chart topper, "Please Please Me," and a revitalized take on Bob's country classic, "Faded Love."

cs

Excerpt from Can't Buy Me Faded Love—The Unauthorized Legend of The Quarrymen, *Ernest and Shultz, 1989*

Looking back, it doesn't seem surprising that those early records found so much success. The world was in love with rock and roll and western swing, and working the two together could only be a recipe for success. But Bob Wills, and more importantly his record company, weren't sure what type of reception these new songs would receive when they hit the record shops. In order to head off any permanent damage to the reputation of Wills' primary band, The Texas Playboys, the label suggested the album be released under a different name. Thus, The Quarrymen were born, and in this initial phase of their existence, the group was marketed as a Bob Wills side project. No mention was made of John's songwriting contributions in the album notes for the first two records, although history has corrected this oversight.

The first two albums, *Meet The Quarrymen* and *Quarrymen For Sale* were modest sellers in the United States and in England, with the single, "She Loves You," enjoying a brief stay on the Billboard Top 20 singles chart. But this moderate success wasn't yet enough to prove the concept to Capitol's record executives. By the end of 1963, a handful of new singles had been released and mostly ignored by the public, and it is unlikely The Quarrymen would have released another album if Bob hadn't pulled the strings to get them the gig that would change the face of music forever.

The Quarrymen played The Ed Sullivan show for the first time in February 9, 1964. Prior to that iconic performance, they were a band at the crossroads and John was a brilliant but unknown songwriter and collaborator, content to live in the shadow of his legendary mentor. But that night changed everything. The Quarrymen became the world's most famous musical group overnight.

And John Lennon became a superstar.

೧೫

Excerpt from Lennon: Honky Tonk Hero, *Lon Haines, 1982*

It was during this rapid onset of stardom that John began to rely heavily on the experience of his better-known collaborator. Although Wills had never enjoyed this level of stardom—indeed, Quarrymania was unlike anything *anyone* had ever experienced—he had enjoyed a great deal of success earlier in his career and understood the responsibility that strolled hand in had with fame. Rather than wilt beneath the weight of public expectations, John took all the support and counsel Bob had to offer.

John credits Wills with "pulling me up by my bootstraps and setting me on the forward path." This perspective allowed John to devote himself to the music, and this is the time when the Quarrymen's two songwriters really began to connect. It is also the time when John began seeing Bob as a sort of surrogate parent, a replacement for and perfect embodiment of the father ideal that he had never known. Despite his subsequent protests in his declining years, it is widely corroborated by band members and personal friends that Wills shared this bond, and treated John as a son. This closeness no doubt contributed to the musical magic, but it made their subsequent sparring more difficult for both.

03

Letter to John Lennon from his Aunt Mimi

August 29, 1964

John,

I was pleased to learn in your recent letter that Mr. Wills has been such a positive influence in your life. Your Uncle and I had occasion to watch your movie. How odd to see your face on such a large scale! What a joy it must be for a boy your age to be besieged by the girls. I only ask that you remember your upbringing and look to Mr. Wills for guidance in matters of propriety. We are proud of you, John! Let us know when we can see you again on the telly.

All my love,

Mimi

൪

Excerpt from an interview with Al Stricklin, Honky Tonk Keys, *December 1979*

"John started smoking pot around the time that *Hard Day's Night* was released. I'm not here to point fingers—half the band at that time was doing the same thing. In fact, I think it was Dylan, the harmonica guy that got him into all that. There was a lot of stress in the air at that time. We put out three records in sixty-four and sixty-five: *Hard Day's Night, Help!,* and *Western Soul.* Add the never-ending tour and two movies, and it all piles up on you quick. John was the biggest music star in the world. Everyone wanted a piece of him. Nobody knows what that kind of fame will do to them until they get it. Some guys in the band hit the bottle, others turned to drugs. The number one rule was, don't tell Bob. He was a drinker, but everyone knew he wouldn't have any of that other stuff in his outfit. So when he found out about John, I was amazed he didn't break up the Quarrymen then and there.

"But, you know, Bob felt like that kid was his son. John's dad left when he was very young, and he'd really latched onto Bob by then. Bob was his idol, his friend, and a replacement Daddy. Bob felt the same way. So when word got out John was into drugs, he took it upon himself to fix the kid. It was going to take more than pot to put a wedge between them two. Yeah, that wedge ended up there, but it took a long while to work itself into place.

"And, you know, the drugs might have started that—Bob got a little more bent out of shape when John moved on to acid. But the whole Jesus thing is what really set the ball rolling downhill."

ߞ

Excerpt from a John Lennon's interview in the London Evening Standard, *March 4, 1966*

"I don't know what will go first—rock, country or Christianity. We're more popular than Jesus now."

ߞ

Excerpt from a John Lennon's press conference, August 11, 1966

Reporter: "Some teenagers have repeated your statements—"I like the Quarrymen more than Jesus Christ." What do you think about that?"

Lennon: "...I'm not saying that we're better or greater, or comparing us with Jesus Christ as a person or God as a thing or whatever it is. I just said what I said and it was wrong. Or it was taken wrong. And now it's all this."

Reporter: "But are you prepared to apologise?"

Lennon: "I wasn't saying whatever they're saying I was saying. I'm sorry I said it really. I never meant it to be a lousy anti-religious thing. I apologise if that will make you happy."

ߞ

Excerpt from Can't Buy Me Faded Love—The Unauthorized Legend of The Quarrymen, *Ernest and Shultz, 1989*

The lion's share of books and articles written about the Quarrymen in the years since the deaths of Wills and Lennon paint

Wills as an "old-fashioned" fuddy-duddy who wasn't hip enough to keep up with his partner's immersion in sixties counterculture. This was hardly the case.

Bob understood the importance of the music they were making, and although John steered the musical direction beginning with the *Colt Revolver* LP, Bob was more than willing to follow his lead. He did not agree with many of John's lifestyle choices—in particular, his experimentation with LSD—but he was quite happy to reap the benefits of those influences. Bob's subsequent love affair with the sitar can be directly attributed to John's study of eastern religions and his time spent under the tutelage of Hindustani musician, Ravi Shankar. And John's descriptions of the aural phenomena he experienced while under the influence of LSD caused Bob to experiment with his fiddle style, ultimately resulting in a new direction in his musicianship, and his still haunting psychedelic fiddle leads on the *Sheriff Emery's Honky Tonk Dive Bar Band* LP.

The fact that Bob continued to embrace these influences in his music after the Quarrymen called it quits in nineteen-seventy is evidence that his interest was genuine. Yet Bob could never reconcile the end with the means. The Quarrymen's recording sessions from sixty-six onward were fraught with strife and electric with tension between the group's two geniuses. It's widely held that this conflict is responsible for the stunning, timeless quality of the recordings produced in this period. John's cynicism about the Vietnam war and the government, amplified by his drug use and declining interest in traditional western swing stood in direct conflict with Bob's more conservative views, and his fear that the music he loved was being replaced by the new genre he'd created.

Each of them viewed the Quarrymen as tool to advance his own agenda, a signpost to direct the masses toward the future of popular music.

It was this collision of wills that created the magic.

ᘓ

Excerpt from an interview with Al Stricklin, Honky Tonk Keys, *December 1979*

"A lot of people have opinions on why the band broke up. But I don't have to guess. It wasn't because John started dating that woman. The drugs and John's lifestyle played a part, I suppose, but the real reason Bob and John stopped getting along was that John lost his love for western music. He started playing his guitar through Marshalls, adding all that distortion that was gaining popularity. It was like rock and roll had been living in his soul all along and now it was clawing to get out. That didn't sit too well with Bob, and it got to where they could barely be in the same room together. Bob would come in of a morning and record his parts with the band, then John would lay down his tracks at night. He was into experimentation by then and Bob would come in the next morning and tape over a lot of what John had recorded the night before. So John would up the ante the next night and the result was *The White Album*. I don't think the two of them spent more than ten minutes in the same room while that one was being recorded.

"The strange thing is, even though John was abandoning his honky tonk roots, there were a whole mess of bands trying to capture that sound he and Bob had made famous. Rock bands like the Byrds and even the Rolling Stones were scrambling to add fiddle parts and lap steel guitars to all their recordings. Bob took it as a compliment, but John resented the whole sixties counter-country movement he'd spawned. He was tired of the whole thing before it even kicked into gear. A whole lot of that resentment comes out on the last few records, especially *Let Me Be*. Bob didn't even want that one released, but John demanded it. He hired Spector to produce it on his own and it hit the stores a full six months after Bob called the Quarrymen quits.

"It says a lot that there ain't one single fiddle part on that record."

◌ß

Excerpt from Lennon: Honky Tonk Hero, *Lon Haines, 1982*

Lennon recalled the dissolution of the Quarrymen and his subsequent feud with Wills with bitter regret. "I was too full of myself, wasn't I? Sometimes I wonder what we could have done with a few more years together. I listen to where guys like Gram Parsons and Clarence White took our music, and I wish now I'd kept pushing the genre. But I wasn't one for listening to criticism and it was easier to throw up my hands and be done with the whole thing.

"But the worst thing is I lost that time with Bob. I spent three years resenting him, and it was like fighting with your father, you know? Maybe some part of you knows he's right but you're too stubborn to admit it. I wish there was some way I could yank the *Imagine* album off the shelves. When I wrote "How do you Sleep," it was obviously a direct stab at Bob and all his lectures on how I was screwing up my life and killing the music I was supposed to love.

"I'm just thankful we reconciled to do that last record. I got to tell him goodbye in my own way."

ᘓ

Excerpt from Can't Buy Me Faded Love—The Unauthorized Legend of The Quarrymen, *Ernest and Shultz, 1989*

Still confined to his wheelchair, and in rapidly failing health, Bob Wills organized what would be his final recording session in December 1973. It was more of a Texas Playboys reunion than anything else, but someone invited John. He showed up in a fringed jacket with a straw cowboy hat leaning to one side of his head, and when he walked into the room, Bob's eyes lit up with tears. Everyone Bob loved and had made music with was there—John, Al Stricklin, Smoky Dacus, Leon McAuliffe—a host of friends and family. But it was John he took aside, and they spent an hour alone, whispering together in a corner, while the assembled musicians prepared to record a selection of Bob's classic songs. The recording session yielded some of the finest recordings of Bob's career, but unfortunately he was unable to participate in the entire event. After retiring on the first evening of recording, Bob Wills suffered his second stroke in four years and lapsed into a coma. His friends, John Lennon included, finished the recording session with tears in their eyes, and what remains is a fitting tribute to a country music legend.

Much speculation has been made regarding John and Bob's final conversation. John described it in numerous interviews as "a heart to heart, between me and my father," but any hope of knowing for sure died with John Lennon's murder in New York City.

Released as *For the Last Time*, the album produced during the last hours of Bob Will's life continues to haunt listeners to this day. His aged, raspy voice can be heard in the call and answer session of "What Makes Bob Holler," and his ever-steady fiddle decorates roughly one-third of the album's tracks. When Lennon takes the vocal lead on "Faded Love" and "A Day in the Life," his voice shakes with emotion. It's an intimate portrait of a man torn apart by human mortality, a shuddering, broken superstar. In the years following Lennon's death, these songs have taken on an added sense of gravity. We know from Lennon himself that he and Wills set aside their differences that day, and became again what they'd once been. Lennon found his father, only to lose him again.

This unlikely reconciliation did more than reunite the greatest songwriting team of the twentieth century. It returned credence to the very beliefs they espoused. For all the turbulence and strife that hounded the Quarrymen throughout their short time together, in the end, they were right about everything.

All you really need is love.

CB

Liner note:

What would have happened if John Lennon left his mates behind in Liverpool, moved to Texas and started a band with western swing legend, Bob Wills? Maybe something like this.

"Can't Buy Me Faded Love" is one of the few stories I've written to fit a title. I was listening to music one day (shock and awe) and I moved from *A Hard Day's Night* to a collection of Bob Wills songs. "Faded Love" kicked in and the title for this story jumped into my head. I couldn't shake the idea and finally it came out over the course of a few days' writing.

I'd never had cause to wonder what a John Lennon country record would sound like—Ringo was primarily responsible for those few Beatles songs that have a country flavor—but all of a sudden it was all I could think about. If Lennon had grown up on western swing instead of Little Richard, maybe he wouldn't have clicked with the rest of the lads in Liverpool. And yet, if his sensibilities remained unchanged from those we came to know, he would never have felt quite at home in Bob Wills' world either. Hopefully this story takes those suppositions to a semi-logical conclusion.

This sold to Eric Marin at *Lone Star Stories*. It was published in the February 2006 issue, and was one of my most well-received stories. Thanks to Eric, and thanks to Bob and John.

Recommended Listening:

The Beatles—*A Hard Day's Night*
The Beatles—*Abbey Road*
Bob Wills & His Texas Playboys—*The Essential Bob Wills 1935 - 1947*
Bob Wills & His Texas Playboys—*For the Last Time*

☙

No One Here Gets Out Alive

There are things known and there are things unknown and in between are the Doors. —Jim Morrison

Zimmerman came to Groover's Paradise with a guitar on his back and a soul full of songs. Doug watched him approach from the east and decided he didn't look like a Nazi. His clothes were little more than artfully arranged rags, and his hair was a wild nest of bouncing curls.

But Groover's Paradise hadn't prospered by taking such things for granted. A Nazi finding his way here was a long shot, but not beyond the realm of possibility. Doug stepped through a stand of cedar trees and blocked the stranger's progress.

"Howdy," Doug said.

The stranger stopped short and fixed Doug with a look that balanced somewhere between confusion and acceptance. "Am I still in New York?"

"Not exactly."

"So where is this place?"

"This place is all over the damn map," said Doug. "If you're looking for a name, we've been calling it Groover's Paradise. How'd you find it?"

"That I couldn't tell you."

"That's normal," said Doug. "What about your name? You remember that?"

"Zimmerman," he said. "I just went out for cigarettes and...shit, where did you say this is?"

"Zimmerman," said Doug. "That German?"

"No. It's American."

"Can you play that guitar?"

Zimmerman ventured a smile. "Can't do much else."

"You hungry?"

"I feel like I haven't eaten in a year."

"Then how about singing for your supper? Something upbeat." Doug wasn't the sort to begrudge strangers whatever food he had to give, but he'd yet to meet a German soldier that knew any good songs. This would be Mr. Zimmerman's chance to prove himself.

Doug watched cautiously as Zimmerman slipped his rucksack to the earth and slung his guitar around in front of him. It was a prewar Martin, the kind they made before the company was taken over by the Reich. The guitar looked tired, just like its owner, but when Zimmerman plucked a few strings, the sound was as sweet and sad as childhood memories.

He broke into a song Doug had never heard before, and Doug couldn't help but smile. Zimmerman's voice was a nasal whine, but he was an earnest son of a bitch. The lyrics bounced around the Martin's steady strum, infused with the purity of truth. There was no guile to this man; he was simply born to make music. The song was ostensibly about the occupation, but as Doug listened, he realized that Zimmerman's lyrics were about more than the crushing realities of post-war American life, and far more than just a series of verses that took satirical stabs at the Germans. Zimmerman's lyrics were a gift. They offered redemption for the oppressed, for those with the right ears to hear it.

Zimmerman ended the song and squinted into the falling sun. "I can play harmonica too. But right now I'd rather eat."

"You write that?" Doug asked.

"Yes I did."

"Come on, then," said Doug, picking up the man's rucksack. "Let's see what's for dinner."

08

Doug led him through the marijuana fields and down a limestone hill that served as the edge of town. Groover's Paradise was a scattering of tents and crooked shacks, laid out with no regard for streets or order. The most extravagant building in town was a two-story log cabin with dark, empty windows. A sign hung over the leaning front door that read MORRISON HOTEL, and the house's owner squatted on the porch, watching them pass from beneath a pair of scratched sunglasses.

"That's Jim," said Doug. "He's been here a while."

Zimmerman waved and Jim gave him a barely perceptible nod of greeting. Shirtless and unsmiling, Jim brushed off his jeans and stood. Lank hair fell to his collarbones, and a mountain man's beard hid his face.

"What's his story?" asked Zimmerman as Doug led him to the fire pit that served as a crude town square.

"Same as everyone else," said Doug. "Got to wandering and he wandered here."

"Do you mind explaining this place to me?"

"Thought you were hungry."

"I am."

"Okay, then let's get some food first."

Janice poked at the fire. She wore a wild dress of threadbare cloth dyed in a rainbow of clashing colors, and her wrists and bare ankles rang with bracelets. Pink feathered scarves tied back her wind-tossed hair. She stood to greet the new arrival when they approached.

"You find a new one, Doug?" she asked.

"More like he found us."

"Well, if he found us, then he's supposed to be here."

Zimmerman introduced himself and Janice gave him a hug. "Take a seat and let's eat. I got some tomatoes and squash that we grew ourselves, and I'm frying up a can of beans that Crosby nicked from a German grocer."

"I appreciate it," said Zimmerman.

They sat quietly by the fire for a time, watching Janice stir the beans and listening to tinny music from her ever-present transistor radio. Static wove in and out of the beat, but Doug recognized Lead Belly's forceful voice warning them they'd better not fight if they ever made it to Houston. Zimmerman hummed along and Doug wondered where he'd heard the song before. There were still American records to be had, prewar recordings that had survived Hitler's culture purge. But they were rare. Doug owned two records—one by the Glenn Miller Orchestra and the other a western album by the Carter Family—and he wouldn't have traded them for anything short of freedom. Not that he had anything to play them on.

Many songs survived in the troubadour tradition, and Doug assumed that's how Zimmerman had come to hear "Midnight Special." Most of Doug's own musical education came from the radio. Not from any of the state run stations, but from the Wolfman. Groover's Paradise was close enough to the border most times to pick up a few stations from Mexico, and the best of them was The X, a high-wattage blast of anti-German propaganda, Delta blues, western standards, swinging jazz and a burgeoning musical style called tejano—a beautiful bastardization of the German's own polka tradition. The man on the radio called himself Wolfman, and he served up daily doses of songs Doug remembered from his childhood. Those songs made him even sadder for the world, and yet some days they were the only thing that kept him going.

He often wondered what kind of music the United States would have produced if the Nazis hadn't put a stranglehold on popular culture. He was envious of the Mexicans and their freedoms. He sometimes thought of swimming south across the Rio Grande, but the fear of SS guns kept him in Occupied America.

"Here you go, darling." Janice handed a plate full of food to Zimmerman, then tossed an empty plate to Doug. "You can get your own."

"You know you love me," said Doug, grinning.

"Yeah, but not enough to scoop your beans." Janice stood and went on her nightly prowl through the camp, rousing everyone from their laziness and summoning them to dinner. Janice and Cass had become the camp's default "women in charge" and they liked to keep things on a schedule. But the population of Groover's Paradise had been steadily growing over the past few years and the ladies' rule was no longer absolute. Some of the folks in camp liked to eat alone and others preferred bootlegged liquor and homegrown drugs to the pleasantries of a social meal. Like most civilizations, their insular world was a steady tension of competing ideals, and Doug had learned long ago that few were willing to bend their wills. They'd all been pulled together here for some reason. But few had much in common.

Doug scooped a small helping of the beans, knowing there wasn't enough to go around, then stabbed a tomato with his fork.

"So tell me about this place," Zimmerman said between bites of beans.

"I'll tell you what I know, which ain't much," said Doug. "I was working in a restaurant in San Antonio, then all of a sudden just felt like I needed out of there. I put down the pot I was scrubbing and walked out the door. Kept going until the town just wasn't there anymore and here I was. A few of the others were already here. Janice. Roky. I think Gram was here too. Anyway, here we were and it just felt like the place we were *supposed* to be."

Zimmerman nodded. "Sounds like what happened to me. And I get the same feeling, like there's a magnet here that attracts the soul."

"Ask around," said Doug. "You'll get the same story from everyone."

"So where is this, exactly? I know you call it Groover's Paradise but where is it on the map?"

"That's just as weird. This place moves around. When I came I guess it was within walking distance of San Antone but then one time me and Cass went walking out past the little creek that cuts through the south end of camp and all of a sudden we're in San Francisco. Right downtown." Doug pointed to the south. "See them magnolia trees over there? Walked through there yesterday and I came to a canyon that fed out onto Sunset Blvd. Hollywood. No telling where you'd end up if you went through there today."

"How'd you get back?"

"If you slip into this place once, you always seem to slip back in."

"None of this makes any sense," said Zimmerman.

Doug shrugged. "You figure out another explanation, I'll listen. What were you doing before you came here?"

"Like I told you. I went out for a pack of cigarettes after a show and all of a sudden the street is gone and here I am."

"Show?" said Doug. "You play music live?"

Zim nodded. "You can still do that in New York. As long as you play music the Nazis approve of. Or if you play in underground places they don't know about. You do that, you'd be surprised the crowds you draw. There's a lot of people out there willing to hear the truth."

"Which truth is that?" asked Jim.

Neither Doug nor Zimmerman had heard him approach. Jim crouched next to Zimmerman, pinning him with that half-crazed, half-genius stare that always gave Doug the creeps. He scratched his beard with the barrel of his .45 revolver and plucked a piece of squash from the plate by the fire. He ate it, grinning.

Zimmerman wasn't fazed by the gun. "The only truth we got. Why go around saluting fascists just because that's the only way of life anyone our age remembers? Things were better before. We're the ones to make it that way again."

Jim shook Zimmerman's hand. "I'm on board with that. World's got too many Nazis."

"I found some more takers on those beans," said Janice. She approached the fire with Duane and Crosby trailing behind her. They gathered around the cook fire and introduced themselves to Zimmerman.

Duane was a wiry man with shaggy blonde hair who spent most days perfecting his slide guitar leads, trying to reproduce from memory the songs they heard on The X. Often a few others would join in with guitars and other instruments while Jim wailed along in his booming voice that was somehow mournful and pissed off all at the same time.

Crosby was a quiet man with a thick moustache and a cherubic face to match his angelic singing voice. He and Doug got along well, but Crosby tended to prefer his own company and it was likely just the lure of a new person in camp that drew him from his tent.

"Thanks for the beans," said Doug, remembering that Crosby had provided them.

Crosby answered him with a lazy smile and piled a plate high with vegetables.

Janice leaned back and took a few swallows from an unlabeled bottle she'd brought with her. It was contraband alcohol, homemade stuff, and though Doug had rarely seen Janice eat, it wasn't often she was found without her bottle. Jim was the same, though tonight he was sober. Focused. All the better to absorb the new guy into his cult of personality. Doug had managed to resist both Jim's militant dogma and Janice's booze. Though he spent more than his fair share of time in the marijuana fields. It seemed most citizens of Groover's Paradise needed some help dealing with their strange existence.

"Did Sir Doug here tell you about this place?" asked Jim. "All the doors, in and out of here?"

"Yes his did," said Zimmerman. "But I still don't get why we're all here and everyone just goes on with their lives never knowing this place exists."

"That's the easy part, man." Jim waved his gun around to indicate all of them sitting there. "This is the melting pot of righteous souls. This is the America that should have been, the people this nation is begging for. The whole county's sleepwalking but us. There's something out there, some great power, some god, whatever you want to call it. And it's put us here together. We've got a destiny of some kind. Mankind needs saviors and here we are! Halleluiah!"

"You ain't no savior," said Duane, grinning. "You *may* be the fucking antichrist."

Jim coughed out a laugh. "Maybe I am. But one way or another, I'm going to make a change in this world. Wasting a gift like we've been giving would be fucking obscene. Like spitting in the face of heaven."

"What gift?" asked Zimmerman.

"The music," said Doug. "Everyone that shows up here can either play the hell out of a guitar or wail like god damn demons."

"Fuck that," said Jim. "I'm talking about the portals that take us in and out of here. Doors to the whole wide world. Think what kind of revolution we can stir up if we mobilize."

Doug put his plate down and sighed. He wasn't in the mood for another of Jim's rants about his revolution. By this point, he could reproduce the loudmouth's nightly tirade verbatim. It was ridiculous to think a misfit gathering of untrained musicians could marshal some kind of armed resistance against the army that conquered half the free world. But when Doug turned an exasperated look in Zimmerman's direction, he was shocked to see the newcomer nodding in vigorous agreement.

"You're right about that," said Zim. "We can change things."

Jim grinned. "One bullet at a time."

For a second Doug had been afraid that Zimmerman was being sucked into Jim's delusions. No matter his faults, the guy had a magnetic personality that sometimes took a force of will to resist. But when Jim spoke, Zimmerman's enthusiasm faded to wariness.

"You think you're going to overthrow the Nazis with force?" Zimmerman asked.

"Force and a hellacious way of getting in and out of town. This place is an assassin's dream. Step through some trees, put a bullet in the Fuehrer's head and be back here in time for dinner. Cause enough chaos and the Reich will go down in flames."

"You're not going to change any minds with bullets," said Zimmerman.

"Don't need to change any minds." Jim stretched out his arm and put the pistol barrel against Zimmerman's forehead. Crosby hissed air through his teeth. Doug froze, afraid he might startle the crazy bastard into pulling the trigger.

Zimmerman's face tightened but he didn't flinch. Jim stared down the barrel at him, unknowable thoughts swimming in his acid-fueled brain. Duane watched with a vaguely interested expression while Janice sat up and held out her liquor bottle.

"Leave him alone," she said. "We all know you're a crazy son of a bitch. You ain't got to prove it. Have a drink and calm the hell down."

Jim ignored her. He kept his eyes locked on Zimmerman and when he spoke his voice was deep and syrupy. "What do you know about truth? Guys like you are afraid of the sacrifices the world demands of its saviors. But here's the thing about fear. You got to face it down. Expose yourself to it. Once you do that it has no power. It shrinks and vanishes. You're free."

"Quit acting like a Nazi and put the gun away," said Zimmerman. "You've let yourself be misled by rage. Killing Germans won't accomplish anything because there are always more of them to fill in the gaps. Besides, half the people out there are so used to the way things are now, they don't have any interest in changing governments. Why the hell step out of line when walking the line ain't so bad? What you've got to do is convince them that it's the worst god damn line they ever saw. Make them realize that what they're living isn't freedom. They don't remember that. You remind them enough and the word will spread. That's how you build a revolution worth having. Change the way people think about their lives. You go in blasting solders and government officials, they'll just think you're some wacko terrorist. And they'll be right."

Doug had been trying to say the same thing to Jim for the last month, ever since he's started talking of guns and killing. But he could never have explained it so plainly. Especially not with a pistol to his forehead.

Jim laughed. "I'm more than a terrorist. I'm the god of sweet fucking revenge." He drew back his gun and stepped away from the fire. Shadows poured down his face like spilled ink. "You sing your songs, little angel. My people are waiting for me deliver them from evil."

He turned and stalked off into the night. Duane stood and followed, casting a look of quiet longing back at the fire.

"What are you gong to do?" Crosby yelled after them.

Jim's self-satisfied voice floated back to them through the darkness. "My mojo's rising, boys. I've got the urge to commit freedom."

ଔ

Zimmerman brought his own kind of magic to Groover's Paradise. Not only did he help Cass in the vegetable garden and pitch in on every chore from scrubbing dishes to digging a second latrine, but his nightly songs were anthems of forgotten freedoms that revealed to Doug part of his own soul he'd never known existed. They had an almost supernatural effect on the attitude of the camp, and Doug came to truly believe that Zimmerman was the final piece of the puzzle, the answer to why they were here.

Doug had given the matter a great deal of thought in the months since Zimmerman's arrived, and though he couldn't subscribe to Jim's ideals, he did agree that sitting around waiting for the world to reveal its answers wasn't the way to go. He was convinced that Zimmerman was right about the music, but less convinced in his own ability to use it as an instrument of change. Zimmerman, though...he was a different story.

He wrote several new songs every day, each one more powerful than the last, and he was attracting a band. One night, Crosby sat in with his guitar and hummed along to Zimmerman's lyrics, chiming in with harmonies as he learned the words. Gram did the same from time to time, and even Cass and Janice joined in when the mood struck them. Doug though about adding his talents to the jam sessions, but he quickly formed the opinion that Zimmerman was one of those rare performers that was best left on his own. No matter what kind of talent surrounded him, it only served to distract from what he was trying to accomplish.

After a time, Zimmerman honed his call for change into an actual plan, and those who shared his opinions, Doug included, fell into a routine of sorts. They spent the evenings studying Zimmerman's song craft and spent the days trying to duplicate it, and they began working on songs of their own, feeling their way through the alien process of speaking their minds through music. For most of them, it came natural, and Doug took this as a sign they were chasing the right goal. They'd been born for this.

When Zimmerman wasn't teaching them his songs, he'd read passages from a road weary copy of Dylan Thomas poems, claiming they were a fine source of inspiration in a world that sorely needed it. The poems always seemed dull and depressing to Doug, but he listened intently, searching for whatever wisdom there was to find.

One night, Zimmerman held court for his growing band of followers in front of the tent he'd fashioned from some oak branches and an Army surplus tarp dotted with bullet holes. He sat cross-legged in the dirt with Crosby. Doug straddled a tree stump. The late hour had chased a few others off to bed.

"I'm aching to play," said Zimmerman.

"You play all the time," said Crosby.

"I mean somewhere else. All I've done since I've been here is talk about kicking this revolution into gear. I figure I've got enough good songs and the rest of you all get where I'm coming from. We need to begin this."

"Tonight?" asked Doug.

"Tomorrow," said Zimmerman. "You take me through one of these doors and I'll get a gig. We find the right city and there's plenty of places that will let you set up and pick a few songs. I'll go first and see what happens. Then we can work up to shows every night. Every one of us hitting a different town, taking the stage and building a movement. The more ground we cover, the quicker we see results. This isn't a quick patch solution. This is gonna take all of our lives and then some most likely. But the road starts here. With this step."

Fall wind hissed through the oak leaves and Doug shivered. He'd heard Zimmerman's plan many times, but the thought of putting it in motion made him nervous. Playing the kind of songs that Zimmerman had been teaching them in a public place was insanely risky. Doug doubted the Nazi police spent much time in nightclubs—particularly since the ban on alcohol for non-German citizens meant they could have more fun in their private clubs—but all it took was a random compliance inspection or one Nazi sympathizer to get them taken out and shot in the street.

Still, Doug was on board with the plan. Any avenue of revolution by nature would involve risks, and he still believed Zimmerman's methods were far superior to Jim's. Zimmerman had proved every bit as magnetic as Jim, and he'd managed to sway some of the wild man's former companions to his way of thinking, not the least of which Crosby, Cass and an experimental guitar player who'd recently arrived named Hendrix.

What Zimmerman had proposed was simple. An army of musicians, all playing the same songs and, regardless of sex, all using the same stage name. It would cement the movement in people's minds, giving the occupying government something to fear and the oppressed Americans a folk hero to rally behind. He claimed to have gotten the idea from a Woody Guthrie album his parents had hidden away and listened to when he was a child. And he'd even rebuilt Guthrie's tune "Pretty Boy Floyd" into an anthem of post-war resistance.

"So what's the stage name?" asked Doug. "You said we'd all call ourselves the same thing."

"Same one I used in New York, I guess." Zimmerman tossed his poetry book down and jabbed a finger at the cover. "I like this cat, and my name's Robert. So when I didn't want anyone to be able to track me down, I called myself Bob Dylan."

"Bob Dylan," said Crosby, grinning. "That's catchy enough. And you really think this will accomplish something?"

"Nothing perks up the oppressed more than the whiff of freedom," he said, picking up his guitar. "If we spread enough of that around, something's bound to happen."

Doug nodded his silent agreement, but he wished he had an idea of what that *something* was.

۸

Word spread quickly that Zimmerman was ready to put his plan in motion, and when Doug met up with him the following evening to help him find a door, a crowd of supporters and detractors gathered to see them off. Jim stood in the middle of the throng, pistol shoved down the front of his pants. Some of his gang surrounded him— Duane and Berry, and a new guy, Lou, with his stoned, thousand yard stare.

Doug hadn't spoken to Jim about his plans since the night Zimmerman had arrived, but the man had been building his own army, and the camp had slowly fractured into two competing revolutions. Newcomers were immediately recruited by both sides, and Doug felt the rampant force feeding of ideals compared unfavorably to the methods employed by their oppressors.

Janice's radio played softly in the distance. A big band song Doug didn't recognize bopped along to the cicada buzz and the crackle of dead leaves beneath their feet. Doug took a deep breath, relishing the scent of cedar and fried eggs. His stomach rumbled in spite of the quick dinner he'd scarfed down, and he wished that he didn't have to take Zimmerman through the door. Groover's Paradise had a lot to recommend it. It was presumably safe from the

32

Germans for one, and more importantly, it was home. If you could convince yourself the outside world no longer existed, it was an idyllic place seemingly painted from Doug's imagination. A haven for free thinkers where his only concern was raising enough food to eat and writing the best damn songs he could. But of course it was impossible to forget about the real world.

Men like Jim and Zimmerman made sure of that.

Doug couldn't hide from his destiny, no matter how much he wanted to.

"Go forth, young warriors," said Jim with a drunken slur. "Ye of righteous cause and stubborn pride. Spread the gospel of steel strings and hollow wood, and deliver your empty gifts bound in pretty paper."

Zimmerman ignored him. "You ready?"

"Guess so," said Doug.

It had been decided that only Doug and Crosby would go with Zimmerman for the first show. Best to use caution the first time out of the box.

Finding one of the doors wasn't a science, more of an instinct. Doug led Zimmerman and Crosby through a patch of mesquite trees and up a small rise that spilled out into the stream that fed through the camp. One of the doors called to him from the edge of the rise and he could tell by the look on Zimmerman's face that he could feel it too.

"Right up there?" he said.

"Yep."

"And no way of knowing ahead of time what city it goes to?"

"Not that I've been able to figure," said Doug. "All I know is it usually spits you out somewhere interesting. Not out in the sticks anywhere, but smack dab in the middle of the action. Shouldn't have to look too hard to find some place to play."

Without another word, Zimmerman took the lead and they followed him up the rise. They stared across the river for a few quiet seconds, then Zimmerman stepped into open air and disappeared. Afraid the door would change on them—in his experience they never led to the same destination for long—Doug jumped after him and Crosby followed.

Right into the heart of an unknown city.

They stood on a brick-covered street crowded with foot traffic, and they hurried toward the sidewalk, trying to blend in with the bustle. Cars crawled past on side streets, and the clean rural air that Doug exhaled was replaced by a thick, smoky substitute that started him coughing. It was always jarring to move from Groover's Paradise directly to a place like this. He winced as a horn blared in his ear, and Crosby pulled him out of the street before someone decided it would be easier just to run him over.

They passed a newsstand and Doug confirmed with a glance at the local paper that this was Boston. Doug glimpsed a sliver of ocean between a pair of smoke-stained buildings, but the city's smog blocked any scent of the sea. He'd never been to Boston before, though he'd seen it in movies before the war. It looked beaten down by comparison, though it was hardly alone in its fate. The Nazi march across the States had begun just over two decades ago, and it had taken them half that time to claim the place entirely. But that was long enough for the nation to take on the dull gray sheen of defeat, and Boston had been under German rule longer than most places.

A tank idled near the intersection, though no soldiers were visible. It was rare any more to find people willing to mount even a token resistance, but the tank remained like a monument to conquest, a steel reminder that Hitler's eyes were everywhere. Doug could practically feel the crosshairs following the back of his neck as they splashed through puddles of brown water and took shelter from a sudden cloudburst beneath a ripped awning.

"This is a likely spot," said Zimmerman, then he pushed through a red metal door. Doug and Crosby followed him into a cramped shotgun bar filled with sallow men, silently nursing dirty glassfuls of beer. Not even the bartender greeted them as they slipped up to the bar. A few murmured comments swirled beneath the squeak of dual ceiling fans, likely comments on their long hair and decidedly rural appearance. But none of the patrons cared enough to give them trouble, and Doug followed Zimmerman nervously across the room.

"These cats don't exactly strike me as music lovers," said Doug.

"This ain't about the music," said Zimmerman. "Never has been." He motioned for Doug and Crosby to take a seat at a nearby table. Doug sank into a sagging chair covered in red velvet and ran his hand across the tabletop, feeling the grooves carved into the wood by beer mugs and pocket knives. A dented metal ashtray spilled over with cigarettes, and one lonely butt floated in a highball glass full of melting ice. Maybe this was the place for Zimmerman to start his revolution after all. A place that served beer and liquor in the open was biding its time, thumbing its nose at the Germans. And the clientele served by such a place had to be halfway suicidal. Men like these had nothing left to lose. Doug could hardly breathe for the desperation in the place.

Zimmerman slid a chair away from the table and into the open at then end of the bar. He sat, rested his guitar across his knee and strummed a chord. The Martin's voice was honey sweet, and Doug wished like he always did that he owned an instrument that fine. The sound raised a few heads, and the conversational tone in Zimmerman's voice when he began speaking caught the attention of the others.

"Hello, friends. My name is Bob Dylan and I'd appreciate your indulgence. I'm in the mood to sing, and you look like you can use a song."

He began a steady strum and Doug felt the hairs stand on his neck. He recognized the song before Zimmerman even began to sing. It was one of his newer songs, a blatant indictment of the Nazis that he called "The Third Reich's A-Gonna Fall." Doug has expected him to ease into things. To get the crowd interested with something less incendiary before baring his soul. But he should have known better. That wasn't Zimmerman's way.

If there had been a German in the room, it would have been within his rights to stand up and shoot the singer where he sat. But there wasn't a German in the room.

These were Americans.

They listened in the same state of dull silence in which they drank their beer, giving no indication that they found the music anything but a temporary distraction from their prolonged state of misery. Zimmerman played on, head down, sweating in the stuffy room as he delivered his truths. He sang like every word pained his soul, and Doug suspected that was the case. When he finished, the Martin left one last resonant note behind, and it hung in the air like a question, waiting on an answer.

It came in the form of soft applause and tentative smiles. Quiet, muted praise. Crosby grinned at Doug from across the table, and Doug felt some indefinable emotion well up inside him. Pride? Terror? It was impossible to tell, but he knew there would be consequences for what they'd done. What Zimmerman had done. He'd started something wonderful, but starting it wasn't enough. Someone, all of them, would have to continue it.

"Thank you," said Zimmerman. He stood, patted Doug on the shoulder and urged him up from the table.

"You done?" asked Doug.

"That's enough," he said, and Doug knew he was right.

They walked together toward the exit, ignoring the bartender's offer of free drinks and the sudden imploring calls for another song. Doug opened the door and let the dim sunlight of the real world back into their impromptu den of resistance. Zimmerman turned back to the crowd, waved goodbye and smiled.

"If you run into Old Man Hitler," he said, "you tell him Bob Dylan says hi."

෬

After that, the revolution kicked into high gear. Zimmerman played a show at least every other night, and others began to follow suit. Doug's first performance was in a grocery store in Philadelphia, and though most of the people picking through vegetables and checking for cracked eggs were frightened off by what he had to sing about, a few remained until he finished. No applause, but something in their eyes told him they understood. The hope in their hearts was a gift from a stranger named Bob Dylan, and they'd pass the name along to their friends, as they passed along his sentiments.

Others met with equal success, though Cass had a close scrape getting out the back exit of a dive bar in Detroit as soldiers beat in the front door. It appeared they were just performing a random liquor raid, but Cass counted herself lucky to have escaped their notice.

The Bob Dylan calling card was a stroke of genius. On both coasts and all points in between, they began to notice graffiti. Walls painted with song lyrics the artist remembered from a show, calling for people to *think* before simply putting their neck beneath the yoke of normalcy and following the Nazi line. Occasionally, they'd encounter singers from the real world performing their songs in basement clubs and back alleys, substituting their own ideas of subversion in place of the lyrics they couldn't remember. But the sentiment was there. The revolution moved slowly, but it *did* move.

Collectively, they'd become the folk hero that Zimmerman had envisioned. But they weren't the only ones trying to change minds.

Jim's revolution picked up steam too, and the evidence of his methods could be seen staining his body every time he returned from the real world. Once a week, Jim and his fanatics would pass through the doors, and return hours later, often covered in blood. Their pistols were Walthers, German salvage pieces no doubt chosen by Jim for their unsettling irony. They'd return waving the guns, eyes glassy from the drugs they took to hype them up for their killing sprees and riding an adrenal rush born of misplaced righteousness. Murder seemed the only thing that could pull Jim from his cabin any more, and Doug worried that his mind was gone completely. Madness and hatred made dangerous partners.

Jim called his travels to the real world *Freedom Attacks*, and the morning after one of his triumphant returns, Doug knocked at the door of Morrison Hotel. He knew that trying to change Jim's mind was foolish, but his attacks were anathema to what Zimmerman's revolution was hoping to accomplish, and Doug felt a crawling certainty that Jim's campaign, if left unchecked, could unravel all the good they'd done.

"Don't bother knocking," said Jim in a lethargic voice. "Come on in."

Doug swung open the door and stepped into Jim's lair.

The room stank of stale sweat and cigarette smoke. Pale light filtered through the ratty window coverings, casting a yellow haze across Jim and his cronies as they lounged on floor pillows with the lassitude of fallen angels with no hope of redemption. Duane and Lou seemed hardly aware of Doug's entrance. They lobbed acid-eyed stares somewhere over his shoulder, as if still wondering who'd knocked at the door. Jim was frying too, but the drugs seemed only to heighten the intensity of his persona. He fixed his gaze on Doug as if peering through his eyes to see what was really going on in his brain.

"Step into my parlor," said Jim, tossing Doug an unused pillow. "Who'd have thought? One of our angelic minstrels, traipsing into the belly of the beast. Have you come to surrender your soul to sweet anarchy?"

"No, I ain't." Doug took an uneasy seat on the pillow, close enough to the door that he'd have a chance to break out if Jim freaked out on him. "Look, man, you've got to quit this shit."

"What shit is that?"

"Killing people. What we're doing, it's working. Word's getting around. People like the songs. More important, they're taking them to heart."

"Bullshit," said Jim. "You don't think I've heard your *songs*? If you insist on music as a medium of societal change, the least you could do is play something with balls. You think you're preaching freedom but the shit you're playing is just more evidence of what's been taken from us. You pick out little folk stories with fairy tale morals so all the dumb ass drunks can understand them. But you're nothing more than crude entertainment for the sheep. You want to stir things up? You need to make some real noise. You need to growl. You need to wail. You want to take those blues songs you can't get enough of on The X and twist them into three minute blasts of pure fucking outrage. You need electric guitars cranked up so high that the speakers can't take the volume. That's how it should have been. I know it, man. I see it. It's like this whole other world just ricocheting around in my head, another life where the music was loud and righteous, and we were free. The world was just as fucked up, but it was the right kind of fucked up.

"So don't crawl in here telling me how Zimmerman's got the masses lining up to march down the happy path to his beautiful new world. There isn't such a world. There never has been, and there never could have been. All we can hope for is a world without Germans in it. Pop, pop, pop, watch them drop. And when the last one's dead, we can peel off the scabs they left behind and see the nice clean scar burned across the face of America. She'll be ugly, man, but it's better than watching her bleed to death."

"You're deluded, man," said Doug. "You haven't seen the look in the people's eyes when something you sing to them strikes a chord in their soul."

"I've seen them," said Jim. "I've probably seen more of Zimmerman's shows than you have. I've watched you, Crosby, Parsons, all of you. I'll give you this. You've got your hearts in the right place. But you ain't making so much as a dent in the German political machine. These people are still buying what Hitler's selling, and what you're offering isn't compelling enough to make them switch brands."

Doug had never seen Jim at one of his performances, but the thought of him straddling the chair at the back of some crowded dance hall, studying him through his aviator shades with those crazed eyes gave Doug the chills. Did he have his pistol with him on those occasions, shoved down the front of his pants for easy access in case the SS decided to crash the party?

"Here's how I know your songs ain't making an ounce of difference. If they were, you'd be dead. The Reich would come down on you like a sledgehammer. A few long-haired peace preachers plucking on guitars in front of a handful of idiots don't mean shit to them. To them, you're not even worth the bullet it would take to shoot you. Me, I got those bastards crawling all over my ass. They don't understand music. They understand pain. That's why your revolution won't amount to shit and mine will."

"You don't know as much as you think." Doug stood, wiped the dirt from the floor off his pants. Trying to talk sense to Jim was a ridiculous notion, but he'd had to try. At least now he could write the man off with a clear conscious.

"How's that?" asked Jim.

Doug opened the door and turned back to face Jim. "Folks know who Bob Dylan is. They tell stories, trying to figure out who he is. They paint his face on brick walls."

"All that's true," said Jim. "But maybe you and the other angels aren't the only Bob Dylan's making a name for themselves in the real world."

"What's that supposed to mean?"

"Let's paint a picture, Doug. Let's say there's this man of ideals and he's got a lot of friends with guns. Well, this man and his buddies they start to make the world a better place by killing the right sort of people. So, maybe they toss a grenade into an SS officer's club, one of those private places, and when they do they shout out something like, "You tell Hitler that Bob Dylan says to kiss his ass." If these men say something like that loud enough that all the people on the street can hear it, well then they can't help but embrace the truth. They do that a few times, show the oppressed how they're just aching to set them free, then all of a sudden you got yourself a bona fide freedom fighter. A folk hero, you dig?"

"You're a son of a bitch, you know that?"

Doug felt suddenly crushed by the hopelessness of it all. What good were all of their dreams with a man like Jim ready to spin them all into nightmares?

"I'm just doing you a favor," said Jim. "Turning up the heat so every one of us understands what's at stake here. It's gonna get so Bob Dylan can't show his face—any of them—between L.A. and New York City without a whole platoon of those lock stepping bastards mobilizing to take him out. That's how we get this thing done. We get them on the run, just like we are."

"I'm not running anywhere."

"Sure you are. We're all on the run. That's how we made it here. That's the fire, swallowing up the world, always a few paces behind. We live in fear. But fear is the very thing that gives us the drive to do what's got to be done."

"Thought you'd mastered your fear."

"I have," said Jim, looking suddenly sad. "But you? Man, you still got a long way to go."

"Fuck you."

Doug walked out into the fading sunlight, chased by Jim's melancholy laughter.

౦ఠ

The revolutions finally collided in Cleveland, at a cramped speakeasy located in the basement of a U.S. war veteran's house. Earlier that night, Zimmerman's daring street corner performance had brought tears to the vet's eyes, and he'd insisted that Zimmerman follow him back to his *club* and play for his friends. Doug was reluctant—they had no proof that the man wasn't a Nazi spy, leading them to their deaths—but Zimmerman agreed and they followed him home. Along the way, Jim materialized from the crowd behind them like the angel of death, come to claim them all.

"You're a fool, Zimmerman," he said.

"What are you doing here?" asked Doug.

Jim shrugged. "I'm a music lover."

The war veteran introduced himself as Alan Freed, and a handful of his invited guests milled around as Zimmerman found a stool in the corner. Alan slid a microphone stand in front of him, and Zimmerman favored him with a curious smile.

"What's that for?" he asked. "I'm pretty loud."

"Figured you might like to expand your reach a bit," said Alan, tapping the microphone. Another man in front of a small mixing console gave the thumbs up sign. "I've got this radio show, see? Strictly under the radar stuff. If the Nazis pinned me down, I'd be thrown under the jail, so keep it all under your hat, okay? I'm always changing frequencies and I never broadcast for more than a few minutes at a time so not much chance of that happening. I don't even know if anyone listens to the damn thing, but I like to think there's somebody out there spinning their radio dial, hoping to catch the broadcast. I usually play contraband records, but you're something new. What you're saying needs to be heard. You don't mind, do you? Just a song, maybe two?"

"I don't mind at all," said Zimmerman. Alan beamed, and he hurried back to the makeshift control booth he'd constructed in the corner of the room with plywood and glass panels. The crowd, four guys who looked less enthusiastic about the music than Alan did, settled into chairs. Doug found an empty one not far from the stage and waited for the show to begin.

Jim prowled in the background, one hand caught in his tangled hair, the other resting nervously on the butt of the pistol protruding from his jeans. He was a man in rapid decline, his cotton shirt so ragged you could see his pale flesh peeking out through the threads, mismatched shoes, one with very little sole left, and jeans stiff with blood he'd neglected to wash away. It was amazing he hadn't been detained just walking down the street. He didn't exactly blend in with the population, and blending in was a necessity.

Somewhere along the line, he'd lost his sunglasses, and Doug wished he hadn't. He didn't like having to answer the questions those eyes posed.

Jim had been tailing them for weeks, slipping into the room just before one of them began to sing. Doug assumed he followed them through the doors when they came to play, and though it made him nervous to spot Jim watching, at least that meant the man wasn't walking the streets, looking for someone to kill. Doug liked to think maybe the music was getting into Jim's soul, a little peace to counteract whatever malignancy had long ago taken hold of it.

But rumors from Jim's crew about their leader killing children and the elderly, railing about them being Nazi whistle blowers, diffused much of Doug's enthusiasm for Jim's recovery. Even Jim's staunchest supporters had begun to distance themselves. They were still hunting Nazis, but with far less fervor. Doug suspected the drugs were no longer enough to ease their guilt, and Jim was doing too good a job of holding a mirror up to their atrocities.

Alan called out for Zimmerman to begin, and he began strumming the Martin. Doug kept an eye on Jim and relaxed a bit when the man quit pacing and began listening to the music. He nodded his head, as if divining some hidden meaning within the melody. Both hands went into pockets, and he leaned against the wall. He was calming down quickly. Losing that dangerous intensity he so often displayed.

Doug tried to shake his nerves and concentrate on the music. Zimmerman's performance was inspired. He was playing one of Doug's favorites, "Masters of War," and his voice carried the heartbreak of their whole lost generation. The kids who couldn't remember life before the war, who had to content themselves with their parent's stories of better days. How could people who'd never known freedom hunger for it so much? Doug had heard the song a hundred times before, but he still felt tears welling in his eyes as the weight of their responsibility came bearing down on him.

Alan and the man helping him with the broadcast were grinning at Zimmerman through a dirty window, and those sitting in chairs watched in polite silence. A tear of memory streaked down one of the men's faces, and Doug knew in that instant that Jim was wrong. They were getting to people. Making a difference in the world.

The man was fishing in his pocket for a handkerchief when his head exploded.

The gunshot was deafening. Before Doug could escape from his chair and hit the ground, the gun sounded again and a second man was dead. The remaining two lunged to their feet, but Jim stood between them and the staircase that led to Alan's garage. Zimmerman had stopped playing, and a stunned silence settled on the room.

The two men put their hands in the air, just like people did in the old movies, and Jim studied them for several seconds before speaking.

"I was blind," he said. "But now I see."

Two more shots and both were dead.

"What the fuck are you doing?" yelled Doug, scooting away across the floor. Jim's maniacal gaze turned his way and he wished he hadn't drawn his attention.

"They were going to bring the Reich down on you. Man, you're too good to live in this kind of world. You guys and your songs. I understand it now, where you're coming from. Fuck all that I said. You're doing a good thing. You're spreading truth. We won't ever be free unless you keep on doing it. No fucking way I'm going to let a bunch of Nazi spies end it. You make the music, and I'll take care that nobody fucks with you for it. A lone devil in service to angels. What do you think about that?"

Jim grinned at Doug, the gun pointed vaguely in his direction. Doug started to protest, but Jim swung his attention to Zimmerman, and when he did, the light faded from his face.

"Aw, fuck."

Doug finally managed to break his gaze away from Jim and saw Zimmerman lying on his back in a pool of blood. The stool lay toppled beside him but his lifeless arms still clutched the Martin to his chest. Doug crawled across the room, intending to perform some kind of first aid before he remembered he had no idea what to do. It didn't matter. Zimmerman was dead, and Doug didn't need a doctor to pronounce him. There was a quarter-sized chunk missing from the top edge of the guitar where one of Jim's bullets chewed its way through before coming to rest in Zimmerman's chest.

"I did not mean to do that." Jim pronounced each word carefully, slowly, as if trying to convince himself. He took no notice when Alan and his engineer bolted from the sound booth and up the stairs. He stared as Doug eased the guitar from his fallen friend's grip and closed the dead man's eyes.

Jim let the pistol fall and it clapped against the concrete floor. He walked slowly to where Doug knelt, pulled the microphone from its stand and lifted it to his lips. Sweat coursed down his face, and his voice shook when he spoke.

"Are we still broadcasting?"

"How the hell should I know, you psycho?"

"Let's assume we are," he said, closing his eyes. "Hello, America. This is the devil, and I've got a message for you. You can't go on living like this. You need to wake the fuck up. I tried to unlock your cages but all I did was bust the key. You're on your own now. I killed your only savior. Bob Dylan is dead."

Jim dropped the microphone and stepped over the dead men. He crossed the room in ominous silence, then climbed the stairs without sparing a glace back.

Doug realized he was on the verge of hyperventilating and he worked to calm himself.

His own freedom became his chief concern as he knelt, shaking in Zimmerman's blood. If the continuing radio broadcast didn't bring soldiers soon, the gunshots or Alan's rapid exit surely would. How long did Doug have before he was sealed in this basement like a tomb? Probably sharing floor space with Zimmerman, a bullet in his head.

His legs seemed hardly able to support his weight when he stood. Standing there, staring down at his friend, he knew that Groover's Paradise was dead. Zimmerman had become the place's soul, and whatever that magic had called them all together for had obviously failed. Like the serpent he was, Jim had ruined their Eden. And though he couldn't have explained how he knew, Doug was certain that the doors going back would be closed to him.

He was numb as he bent over and lifted the guitar. Despite the bullet hole, it was still in reasonable shape, and Doug couldn't imagine leaving such an artifact for the Nazis. Zimmerman's blood coated it, but Doug made no effort to clean it off. Maybe some part of him would stay with the instrument, just as his ideals stayed in the heart of Doug and Crosby and Janice and all the others. Zimmerman was gone, but Doug wasn't. Groover's Paradise was a great place to hide, but it wasn't necessary. Doug had a guitar and he had the songs. That's all he really ever needed.

He slung the guitar strap across his shoulder and made for the exit, unsure what would be waiting for him in the real world above. He had to find a new home. And most of all, new minds to change.

Groover's Paradise was dead.

But Bob Dylan was still very much alive.

ભ

Liner notes:

If you've never heard of Doug Sahm, he's the best rock and roll, tejano, blues, jazz, country, psychedelic R&B singer, fiddler, guitar player ever to groove vinyl.   The man was an encyclopedia of musical styles and he excelled at every one, generally mixing them together into an unmistakable sound that was purely his own.

Doug began appearing on the radio at age five, made his first record at eleven, and even took the stage with Hank Williams just weeks before the famous country singer's death. He spent time in the Haight-Ashbury scene with his band The Sir Douglas Quintet, and spent the next three decades releasing solo projects and playing with various incarnations of his older bands.

I'm a fan of everything he's done, but the sweet spot is probably the sessions he did with Jerry Wexler for Atlantic Records in 1973. Bob Dylan and Dr. John were in the mix and the result is something really special. Two albums resulted from this period, <u>Texas Tornado</u> and <u>Doug Sahm and Band</u>. If you can find either of them, they're certainly worth a listen.

I'd wanted for a long time to write a story about people who would have been rock stars in our universe, fighting fascism in a Nazi occupied America. What form would the music and the rebellion of the sixties have taken under those circumstances? And how would the folkies and the rockers have co-existed? Doug was a friend of Dylan, and when Zimmerman stepped onto the scene the whole thing started coming together for me.

Recommended Listening:

The Doors—*Morrison Hotel*
Bob Dylan—*The Times They Are A Changing*
Bob Dylan—*The Freewheelin' Bob Dylan*
Doug Sahm—*The Best of Doug Sahm's Atlantic Sessions*
Sir Douglas Quintet—*The Best of the Sir Douglas Quintet*

Gifting Bliss: Fifteen Years Later, Jason Avery's Magic Is Still Saving the World

It's hard to imagine that fifteen years have passed since the release of *Gifting Bliss*, a record that as of this writing has sold more than eleven million copies and continues to sell several thousand copies per week. This is a testament to the fact that Jason Avery's brand of riotous music and broken-soul lyrics remains vital and relevant, even though the spells his songs cast have long ago followed their creator into the realm of legend.

The rabid fans that propelled *Gifting Bliss* into a worldwide phenomenon have grown beyond the adolescent angst that fueled the band. Yet they remember a time when the magic contained in rock and roll was just a metaphor, and they remember when a band called Broken showed them it was something more.

In the wake of their debut album, *Scorch* (Sub Art, 1989), Broken was a band looking for a direction. Loved by the local Dallas music scene but mostly unheard of beyond the dive bars populating Deep Ellum, *Scorch* was a collection of three minute aural assaults— bare toothed guitar riffs influenced as much by the heavy metal that Avery claimed to hate as it was by bands with more indie cred like

Wasted Sound and The Prix. By all accounts, Avery was never happy with the heavier musical direction original drummer Chris Stein wanted to pursue and was unhappy when it manifested itself during recording. "I started the group, right?" said Avery in a 1993 interview with Urban Guitar. "And I didn't set out to be in a metal band. I wanted heavy, but I wanted a different kind of heavy."

This disparity of musical ambitions led to Stein's departure not long after the album's release. After a series of replacements fell flat, Avery and bassist Tom Silvering invited Michael Grip, drummer for the recently dissolved Dallas band, Thud, to join the band. It's this lineup that Broken fans are familiar with, and this lineup that entered Sound City Studios in the San Fernando Valley to record the album that changed the world.

Two years of brutal touring had yielded little commercial success, but Griffin Records A&R man Mark Kloss got wind of Broken when they played New York's notorious Shambles Club, and decided to put them in the studio and see what happened.

Kloss believes the famed Broken magic was on display that night. "You could feel something weird in the club. That Shambles show, that was the first time I felt it. That *tingle*, you know? How we all came to feel the magic when it was kicking in? It wasn't what it would be, but it was there. I had no idea, of course, what I was feeling. But I knew enough to figure this band was special."

In May 1990, Broken entered the studio with producer Alan Ash, whose work with underground bands like Stack Acid and The Bittering had earned him a rep as someone willing to push musical boundaries. Broken agreed with Griffen's choice of producers, one of the few matters on which they'd see eye to eye in coming years. Ash, however, wasn't entirely prepared for the band's approach to recording.

"First time I met Jason he was sitting cross-legged in the middle of the studio, surrounded by burning candles. The air smelled like flowers and a sort of fog hung in the room and I'm thinking this dude is a little off. He's got his guitar in his lap and he's chanting. We were there for a preproduction run-through of the songs, just a way for me to get a vibe for the music, and already the guy seems like a flake. I asked Michael what Jason's doing, and he gave me this weird smile and said, 'casting spells.'

"I blew it off as eccentricity. When they kicked into a run-through of 'Tastes Like Mommy's Lies,' I forgot about it completely. God, that song! Imagine hearing *that* song for the first time, not on the radio but right in front of the guys playing it. I knew straight up it was gonna be a hit, and all of a sudden I forgot about my hangover and I'm bouncing around the room, getting into the spirit. Weird, but it didn't occur to me until long after 'Tastes' became a hit that it probably cured my hangover that day."

"Tastes Like Mommy's Lies" was the first song put to tape during the recording sessions, a brutal nest of buzzing guitar chords that somehow still rang with poppy hooks. The song's frank lyrics decried the failures of the Baby Boomer generation and the fallout it wreaked on their children.

Avery's detachment from the world in the wake of his parents' divorce at age seven is well documented, and his musical output stands testament to the fact that he never recovered. When he sings Join with me / bleeding kids / Don't believe / what family is, the listener can't help but feel the pain of the child inside the man. His voice is coarse, strangled with history, and yet still vulnerable.

It is even more unbelievable, then, that such a cry of anger could yield such a wonderful bounty. It's as if Jason Avery used his own pain to power the magic in his music, and by flushing it from himself and out into the world, it's rendered into something more benign. The power to heal. The power to make dreams real. The power to save lives.

Michael Grip, now the frontman for Fabulous Crash, never understood his bandmate's magic, but he knew its source. "Jason wasn't too happy, even then. He'd set up all these candles before we recorded a song. Then he'd scribble all these symbols on the walls, weird shapes and stuff that looked like it was in some alien language. Then he'd howl, just fucking wail, you know? Like he was purging everything he was pissed off about from his soul.

"He told me one day when we were recording *Gifting Bliss* that he wanted the record to change the world. To make it better. He wanted it to fulfill all the peace and love dreams the sixties had promised. Said he felt like we were supposed to be living a better life, and we'd been cheated."

One of the true ironies of Jason Avery's life is the fact that his mother taught him his spells. He rarely spoke of this, but in an unusually candid interview in 1994, just a month prior to his death, Avery said he should have given his mother a songwriting credit on most of his songs. "She was into all that weird shit and she taught me. I never wanted anything to do with magic until I figured out it could make music sound better. Everything else was just a side effect."

Hardcore fans still like to believe that Avery knew exactly what he was doing when he enchanted bits of his soul into songs like "Tastes," "Hang You," and "Anti-Depressant." All three created a wake of miracles that many more pragmatic members of the public still refuse to believe took place. But by Avery's own admission, the magic was only supposed to improve the music, not make it spiritually transcendent.

Ash and the band wrapped recording on *Gifting Bliss* in June 1991 and after several months of post-production, it was released to the public on September 24, 1991. But even before its release, word of the soon to be legendary album had spread widely though the recording industry. Record company executives, board engineers, and various members of the growing Broken entourage began reporting strange occurrences while listening to the music: old injuries healed, unheralded blasts of creative inspiration, tiny miracles with no explanation, all tied together by one rock and roll record.

Broken began a European tour the same week that *Gifting Bliss* was released in America. As the record grew in popularity and word about what was happening spread slowly to the mainstream, the crowds they attracted grew exponentially larger.

"That's when Jason decided to work his magic into the shows," said Michael Grip in a 2003 interview with Contemporary Drummer magazine. "People were digging the fact that the music was working on them. Causing them to feel some real peace, curing their grandma's asthma. Whatever. So when that didn't happen at the shows, it was sort of a letdown. The music by itself wasn't enough.

"That bugged the shit out of us, so Jason decided to do something about it."

Broken first used live magic during a concert in Brussels, Belgium on December 19, 1991. The band was late in starting and the crowd grew restless, but none realized the delay was due to Avery calling on his angst, forging it into something wonderful. His gift of anger. By all accounts, it was a blistering set, but the glory of the music itself is almost forgotten in the wake of the miracles it spawned that night. Twenty thousand fans entered the arena with the common pains and maladies of humanity—injuries, diseases, mental illnesses—and when the concert was over, twenty thousand people left these problems behind. They were cured, and though few who weren't there were willing to believe such a miracle, the truth would soon win out. The Brussels show was just the first of many such performances.

Upon their return to the United States, Broken was astonished at its own popularity. A US tour began in the spring of 1992 and shows sold out far in advance. Word of the Brussels miracle had spread, and Avery was obliged to bring magic into more and more live shows.

"He didn't always work the spells before the shows," said Grip. "It took a lot out of him. But when he did, the results were amazing."

Fans flocked to the shows, many just in hopes of being healed. The music fixed everything: cancer, AIDS, heart conditions. Those who left with their miracles in hand became fans for life. Those who left without them often felt cheated, and small-scale riots were not uncommon.

Avery had a hard time understanding this backlash. "I can't work the magic every night, okay? I've said that publicly. It takes something out of you, and whatever that is, it's not in unlimited supply. I made a record. We made a record. You can buy a copy whenever you want and most of these people bitching already have. That's my soul right there on the disc. So what if the record just cures headaches or makes you feel kind of peaceful? Kind of high? So what if it doesn't make you jump up out of your wheelchair and walk? That's good fucking music and it means something. I'm a guitar player. I didn't sign on to be the world's savior."

His confusion turned to resentment near the end of his life, when he was famously quoted in an MTV interview. "Fuck the ones that only care about the magic. I care about the music. I don't fucking need fans like that."

But the more people who were healed by Broken's music, the more it was expected of them. The pressure to bring the magic to bear each night was intense, and Avery was showing signs of breaking. Stories of heroin use and several near death overdoses leaked to the press. But this garnered no sympathy for rock and roll's messiah. Instead, it created an even more fervent demand for his gift. Fans were terrified that he'd die before they were able to experience it for themselves.

Broken entered the studio in March 1993 to record the much awaited follow-up to *Gifting Bliss*. The result was a chaotically beautiful record full of wry lyrics and growling guitars. *Take No More* was released to mobbed record stores on September 21, 1993, but Jason Avery had once again defied fan expectations.

He'd entered the studio without his magic.

Take No More was an indictment of the fans who'd used him for their own gain. Though the music was even heavier than the earlier Broken albums, Avery's anger was far less focused. *Take No More* was the product of a songwriter coming to the realization that no matter what he'd achieved, he was just as doomed to failure as the older generation he resented. What he had to give the world, however extraordinary, would never be enough.

Fan reaction to *Take No More* was mixed. Most agreed that the songwriting had grown even stronger, but those who worshipped the magic edged toward revolt. Jason Avery was still letting the world have his music. But he was keeping the magic for himself.

Never was this more apparent than his final live appearance, Broken's legendary MTV Unplugged performance just a month prior to Avery's death. Stripping away the searing guitars that drove their music, and with Avery's magic conspicuously absent, Broken played a transcendent mix of hit songs and cover tunes that proved once and for all that they were one of the finest rock and roll bands ever to take the stage, with our without enchantment.

Avery appeared to be a man finally at peace with his place in the world, able to accept the magic that overshadowed his music and to move forward on his own terms. All throughout Broken's final tour, he'd kept the magic at bay, and though many fans couldn't understand why he'd keep it from them, this final performance at last forged an understanding between the would-be messiah and his followers. Jason Avery had no magic left for the world. But his music was enough.

"I've never been so excited about a show," he said in the wake of the MTV performance. "No wall of noise, no magic. Just us. Three guys making music and making people smile. What the fuck is better than that?"

Jason Avery seemed to have made peace with his world, but one month later, he was dead.

His body was found in his North Dallas mansion in April 1994. No cause of death was immediately apparent. Lying on the bedroom floor, arms wrapped around his acoustic guitar, it appeared to investigators that he'd simply died while playing. Further investigation turned up the tape recorder he'd used to record his last hour on earth, and though it could not be medically proven, it was finally determined that Jason Avery had committed suicide.

This tape was never released to the public in its entirety, though bootleg recordings of that final song are readily available on the internet. In a strained voice, Avery delivers his farewell to the world, "One more time with the magic," then begins to strum. One can almost picture the candles burning in a circle around him, the runes, the cryptic drawings and other bits of mystic arcana that he used to fuel his music, all with him at the end.

Listeners claim this last song can bring on headaches, grow tumors, spread disease. Regardless of whether this is the case, the magic in the song came from a darker part of Jason Avery's soul, a place filled with self-loathing and perceived failure.

The magic in Broken's records still lives. Every year more fans discover its healing properties and the way it seems to cleanse the soul. We're left to wonder what new musical magic Avery might have created had he not taken his life. But Jason Avery will forever be defined by three years of stunning rock and roll that changed the world. And despite his best efforts, history won't remember the man Jason Avery wanted to be, but the man he was.

Hopeful. Brilliant. Broken.

We still have the music. And for most, that's enough.

ↂ

Liner notes:

This follows the path of one of the more well-known rock and roll stories of the early nineties. It was inspired by an article in Spin magazine a few years back memorializing the tenth anniversary of Kurt Cobain's death. Every person and every band in this story has a real world analog, and it shouldn't take much digging to figure out who they are.

There was certainly some kind of magic in that music, but as far as I know, none of it was the real thing.

Recommended Listening:

Nirvana—*Nevermind*

Nirvana—*In Utero*

Nirvana—*MTV Unplugged in New York*

The Pixies—*Doolittle*

Sonic Youth—*Goo*

ↂ

Stephanie Shrugs

Stanton, TX— October, 1989

It's easy to get girls when you play guitar.

At least in a nothing town like mine. The kind of place people from the city drive through and wonder how anybody could live there. Nothing for a sixteen year old to do but get drunk and find trouble. Not that I'm complaining. Fill a Big Gulp cup half full of Coke, then top it off with a pint of Jack and life gets better in a hurry.

My friend Bobby's garage is insulated well enough that our band can usually jam for a couple of hours before the cops show up, and that's what we're doing when this woman walks in.

I'm not talking about one of the high school girls that lounge around on the stained orange sofa we keep in the corner, sucking on bottles of Strawberry Hill. Most of them think I'm a rock star.

But this is a *woman*. Early twenties probably, and gorgeous. She's got killer hair, an explosion of blonde curls falling down her back. A Whitesnake tee-shirt, tiny denim skirt studded with silver. No way she's from around here. The town's small enough that you get to know everyone, for better or worse. And besides, she's made for MTV. Last I checked, they aren't shooting any rock videos in the Dairy Queen parking lot.

I'm choking out the lyrics to "Youth Gone Wild"—not that I'm much of a singer, but I'm doing my best—when I feel the vibe change in the room. All eyes, mine included, lock on the woman as she takes a few steps into the garage and lights up a cigarette. You can tell straight off all the girls hate her. Catty foreheads pressed together, lips hidden behind their hands, nervous laughter. Probably talking about what a slut she is.

Our jam sessions attract guys too. A few friends, always ready for a party, and a bunch of guys who aren't part of our crowd but would like to be. They look all serious and nod their heads, like they're really into the music and too cool to bother with the girls. Meanwhile they're wondering if they have a shot at getting laid, and telling themselves they're finally gonna buy a guitar and learn to play. Can't be that hard, right? But none of them ever will.

That's the difference between us.

Now they're staring at the woman, trying not to look like their minds are totally blown, trying harder than ever to seem cool. And I realize I'm doing the same damn thing.

We finish the song and there's some restrained clapping from the guys, a few hoots and whistles from the Strawberry Hill section.

"I need a beer." I slip the guitar over my head, place it gently on its stand. My fingertips ache and I love it. My heart's thumping like a Metallica riff, and I'm not sure if it's the adrenaline or the fact that a woman who should be hanging on my bedroom wall is standing in Bobby's garage, staring at me. But she might as well be the plague. The girls won't have anything to do with her, and the guys know she's way out of their league. Mine too, but I guess she hasn't figured that out. While I'm digging a beer out of the cooler, trying not to stare, she makes her move.

"Got something for you," she says.

I stand up, pop the tab off the beer and offer it to her. I hope my hand isn't shaking too much.

She shakes her head and reaches into her bag. "No thanks. Just came to give you something."

She smells like some kind of berry, one of those perfumy soaps girls use, and it starts to drive me a little crazy. Then she places a record album in my hand.

"What's this?" My best "too cool to care" tone.

"Look at it."

I do, and it's just a normal record. The cover is a black and white photo, a reverse negative of some long-haired dudes rocking out. Looks a hell of a lot like every other garage band on the planet. The album's called *Bleach* and the band's named Nirvana.

"Yeah? Who're these guys?"

"Nirvana."

"I can read. But what's this for? Why're you giving it to me?"

She leans in so close I can feel her earrings against my cheek. Her whisper is warm in my ear. "Because it's going to change your life."

She pulls back, kisses me right on the corner of my mouth. Before I can recover from my mini heart attack and figure out how to respond, she's ducking beneath the half-open garage door.

A second later, she's gone.

Realizing everyone's staring at me, I chug the entire can of beer and strap on my guitar like it was no big deal.

Later that night, I drop the needle on the record.

And my whole fucking life changes.

ೞ

Seattle, WA— October, 1993

It's easy to get coffee when you live in Seattle.

French roast, espresso, latte, some frothed something or other topped with whipped cream. Might as well be a milkshake. Me, I'm drinking plain old American Joe—black—watching rain streak down the window.

The place is called *Bean There, Done That* and it's homey. One of those little hole-in-the-wall dives that makes you feel like a local just because you know it exists. I guess that's what I am now, a local. Been here a couple of years and people have mostly stopped commenting on my Texas accent. My coffee cup's empty and I'm trying to decide if I have time for another before rehearsal. I've been stalling, hoping the rain would stop. I should know better.

The brass bell over the door rings. I look up, and there <u>she</u> is. I haven't seen my mystery woman since the night she turned me on to Nirvana, set me on the path that ultimately led here. Different hair, different clothes, but nothing else has changed. She's still a knockout, like she hasn't aged a day. Obviously the woman's a few years older than me, but she doesn't look it. She doesn't have to scan the room; she already knows where I'm sitting. I'm not surprised when she takes a seat at my table.

Her jacket's denim, her tights are some sheer black fabric, her skirt's tie-dyed cotton. The blonde curly hair doesn't have nearly as much hairspray, but it's just as beautiful. So's her voice. "I knew you'd be here."

I laugh, wondering whether she means *Bean There, Done That* or the state of Washington. Wondering whether that even matters.

"Was I right? Did the record change your life?"

I nod. She already knows it did. "What's your name?"

"Stephanie."

Her name yanks me from the overcast world of today and drops me smack dab in the middle of memory. A weedy, elementary school playground, sitting with Stephanie Warner on a bench built to look like a caterpillar. Green paint chips flake away as she scoots closer to me, then plants a kiss on my cheek. Her lips rest there for two wonderful seconds and a whole new world of possibilities is born in my mind. Then she takes her lips back and runs away. I realize how much Stephanie Warner reminds me of the Stephanie sitting across from me. She smiles, and I get the uneasy feeling she's sharing my memories.

"I like that name." A day hasn't passed in three years that I haven't thought about this woman, and that's the best I can muster. I'm so overloaded with questions, I don't even know where to start. Just like last time, Stephanie leads the way.

"You're wondering who I am."

"For starters."

"And whether or not I'm an escaped mental patient."

I laugh. "The thought had crossed my mind."

"You tired of Garageland yet?" Her question comes straight out of left field and I'm not sure exactly what she means.

"The song? Shit no. The Clash never gets old."

"Not the song, the lifestyle. Wake up, go to your suck day job, then jam in somebody's garage, or somebody's cousin's rented rehearsal space. Then on weekends you scramble for third bill at a bar you've never heard of, just so you can make no money and do it all over again. That's Garageland. You tired of it?"

"At least I'm doing something I love."

"So you wouldn't rather do something you love *and* get paid for it? Your band is good enough. All that's holding you back is contacts. You don't know the right people."

"I know the guys in Nirvana." I'd moved to Seattle right after graduation, and met Kurt Cobain just a few months before everybody on the planet figured out who he was. Good guy, pretty shy actually. Now he's been harnessed with a level of fame I can only imagine. I haven't seen him in over a year.

"Good for you. How many gigs has that gotten you lately?"

"Not many."

"You want to headline?"

"Of course.

"Then call this guy." She hands me a business card with a booking agent's name and phone number on it. Before I can tell her I've hounded every booking agency in the Northwest, she starts talking again. "Invite him to your next gig. He'll pay you lip service, then hang up on you. But he'll be at the gig. Play your ass off. If you do, it'll change your life."

She pushes her chair back and stands.

"Hang on," I say, not comfortable enough to grab her arm, but desperate to keep her from walking away again. "Where are you going? Do you live around here?"

She shrugs her shoulders and smiles. "Chill out. You'll see me again. Probably." She gives me another kiss, and this one lingers on my lips even after she pulls away. I can't do anything but watch as she walks out of the coffee house. I want to follow her, but I'm afraid of what might happen if I do.

The business card is like an unfulfilled promise in the palm of my hand.

She was right last time.

"That a public phone?" I ask the waitress cleaning off the table next to me.

"Sure, if it's a local call."

It's hanging by the door. I have to pass it before I brave the rain.

"Fuck it," I say, and dial the number.

ᴄ8

Seattle, WA—April, 1994

It's easy to kill yourself with a shotgun.

Just ask Kurt.

Stick it in your mouth and pull the trigger. Nothing left but an ugly stain to clean up, a generation of people blindsided by reality, and one bona fide rock and roll legend.

Too fucking easy.

Rain pours from the sky like it always does, but nobody gathered at the makeshift memorial gives a shit. They're all too stunned. Plenty of tears and mumbled prayers. Ink smearing on condolence cards, wilting flowers, crushed cigarette packs, beer cans. Disillusioned, muddy mourners. Some guy with an acoustic guitar keeps playing "All Apologies" over and over again, like it's going to change anything. He'd better stop soon or I'm gonna knock the shit out of him.

My anger surprises me. Something like this, you figure I'd be sad. But instead, I'm pissed. What was the guy thinking? I knew about his drug problems and his screwed-up personal life. But I can't imagine it getting to the point where somebody decides to end it with a shotgun blast. Kurt was the biggest rock star in the world. The guy had a kid, for God's sake.

A few of the guys in my band were here earlier, but the rain chased them away. Me, I'm here for the long haul. I'm looking for some kind of understanding.

Stephanie appears next to me, and I realize I've been expecting her to come.

She looks no different than she did that day in *Bean There, Done That*, except now she's wearing a bright yellow rain slicker. Her hair is pasted to her skull, just like the rest of us. She laces her fingers through mine and leans her head on my shoulder.

"Why'd he do it?" There are so many other things I'd like to ask her, but none of them seem important right now.

Stephanie shrugs. I don't expect anything more. I gave up trying to understand her a long time ago. Stephanie is Stephanie. She just *is*.

"You heard my song on the radio?"

"Of course," she says.

Stephanie's advice had been dead on. The booking agent was an asshole, but he loved us. Got us gigs at all the cool clubs and we wound up signing with Sub Pop. We've been getting some pretty good local airplay. Nothing major, but we're famous enough around town that quite a few of the mourners recognize me.

"What are you here for this time?"

She looks into my eyes and her usual amusement has been replaced with sadness. "You sure you want this?"

I'm used to her answering my questions with questions, but I don't know what she means by *this*. "The fame or the suicide?"

She doesn't answer, she just keeps staring.

"Look, I love Kurt but the guy obviously had problems. If you're asking whether I want to give up my dream of being a rock star, the answer is no. It's all I ever wanted. My head's on straight."

"I'm not saying you'll kill yourself. Just that not every dream is worth falling asleep for."

"I'll take my chances."

"Then think of me, next time you write a song."

"Let me guess. It'll change my life."

"Hopefully not too much." Stephanie kisses my nose, then disappears. I don't mean she gets lost in the crowd. She just fades away, and so does any pretense that she's a normal person. Not that I hadn't already figured that out.

A melody pops into my head. Something radio-friendly but not so much it makes me feel like a sell-out. I think about the sadness in Stephanie's eyes, and the coy way she shrugs her shoulders. I think about how beautiful and strange she is.

And the lyrics come in a torrent of inspiration.

Stephanie Shrugs

଼

New York, NY—March, 1999

It's easy to lose perspective when you're the biggest rock star in the world.

It's also easy to lose hope.

I stare out the window of my New York penthouse, past the jagged landscape of skyscrapers, to the far horizon. Somewhere out there is Bobby's parents' garage, and I wonder if it's changed. Could be they've converted it into a workshop or filled it with all the junk they don't have room for in the house anymore. Maybe just parking their cars there like normal people. But I like to think it's still the same. Amps humming, a skinny kid smacking the snare drum, impatient for the song to start. Another one tuning a hand-me-down guitar. The place clogged with cigarette smoke and laughter.

That's what it's about, right?

Rock and roll. Not rock stars.

I'm alone, thank God. Finally ushered out all the people with their hands in my life, the ones pulling the strings and the ones just content to push me closer to the edge. People who only want to be near me because I'm famous. They don't care about me, and the feeling's mutual.

I don't even turn around when I see Stephanie's reflection in the glass. But I smile. I used to think my unhappiness was Stephanie's fault. But she's never done more than give me what I wanted most in the world.

"How's the dream?" She comes into focus and she's standing beside me. She still smells like berries, and she's still painfully beautiful.

"Not bad. It has its rough edges, but it beats living in obscurity." I only half believe my own words.

"Glad to hear it. 'Stephanie Shrugs,' huh?"

"Not a bad name for a song." Not a bad name for a cultural revolution either. "Stephanie Shrugs" launched us from nightclubs to stadiums. It was the kind of song you can't escape. Airport lobbies, restaurants, elevators. Every fucking station on the radio dial. The album hugged the top of the Billboard charts for two years. Even my grandma bought a copy.

"Just before your CD hit the charts, I gave a copy of it to this kid living in Garageland. Changed his life."

My smile fades. "You did, huh? Didn't know you got around that much."

The realization that I share this vision with someone else causes me to feel betrayed. Jealous even. Ridiculous, but I can't help it. I've seen this woman a handful of times in my life, but I'd convinced myself she existed *for me.* I'd even entertained thoughts that one day she'd stay. How can someone who's so fleeting be the most important person in your life?

Stephanie shrugs, and I've never been so hurt in my life.

"Why are you here? Do I need you anymore?"

The pain in her eyes immediately makes me regret my words. A face like that isn't supposed to hurt.

"I came to see if you were tired of this yet."

"How could I be?"

I can tell she wants to shrug, but she thinks better of it. "It can be a little much."

"I'm fine. You can stop worrying. Anything else?"

Stephanie shakes her head. She's stopped looking me in the eye.

"Then have fun with your new pet project."

Stephanie steps through the glass and vanishes into the New York night.

She doesn't bother to kiss me this time.

ଓ

Dallas, TX—April, 2004

It's easy to contemplate suicide when you're this fucking lonely.

Bottle of sleeping pills, straight razor to the wrist—lengthwise, not across—a noose dangling from that gigantic oak in the backyard, Drano cocktail, stepping in front of a bus. Doesn't matter. It all ends the same way.

Christ, how did I get here?

My North Dallas home is cluttered with junk. Unwashed dishes; stacks of CD's removed from the rack and left on the coffee table, couch, kitchen table, bookshelves, floor; way more guitars than any human needs, a drum set, a whole wall of amps; half-empty beer bottles by the score; a half-smoked bag of weed; me. Barefoot, torn jeans, shirtless.

In the middle of it all, I see the latest issue of Spin. A commemoration—ten years since Kurt's death. All that time, but he's still staring at me, and those eyes don't offer any answers. But the journalists think they have him figured out. He wasn't built for fame. The drugs, the upheaval, the way every person you meet wants to be *right fucking next to you*. Wants to touch you, wants you to say something cool they can tell their buddies about, wants you to *see* them, with *those* eyes. So all the pressure drove him to heroin, misery, depression. Death.

I'm not mad at Kurt anymore. I think I understand why he did what he did.

The thing is, Kurt never got to find out what life's like on the other side of the rollercoaster. When the sales begin to slump and the record label drops you. When all your friends find new friends, and all the skinny tan twenty-somethings in their hip hugger jeans and belly shirts find a new God to worship. When nobody gives a fuck about any of your new music because it's not "Stephanie Shrugs." When you realize they're right and your muse has abandoned you.

When you're so in love with a mystery you can't even function.

The place smells like an ashtray and so do I. I've cleared just enough space on the carpet for me and the shotgun. It's an old Remington my granddad used to hunt quail with and I figure if it's good enough for Kurt, it's good enough for me.

I take a drag off my cigarette and think about the way Stephanie looked the first time I saw her. The way she'd look now if I hadn't chased her away. Would I have really been better off working in my Dad's video store for the rest of my life, marrying the best woman I could find in a town that small, letting a couple of kids put my dreams on hold? Maybe. Probably not. But it doesn't make today any easier to live with.

My face is wet and I realize I'm crying. No one to be cool for, so I let them come. The tears, the heaving sobs, all building toward the resignation I'll need to pull the trigger.

Somewhere, "Stephanie Shrugs" is playing on the radio.

Then I feel her arms wrap around my bare shoulders, her kiss on the back of my neck. I smell berries and second chances. No way I can hold back the tears now. My whole body shakes, and I can't even face her.

We sit there for an hour, silent. Contemplating one another. Then Stephanie stands and I look up at her for the first time. I'm older than she is now. She's wearing jeans and a loose-fitting Get Up Kids tee-shirt, tucked in. I can't help but smile.

She doesn't speak, but she offers me her hand.

I take it without hesitating, and pray to God she's going to change my life one last time.

 og

Garageland -- November, 2006
It's easy to find Garageland again, when your muse leads the way.

Different garage, same concept. I even have an ugly old couch. Of course, I'm a little more high-tech now. This garage isn't just a place to jam, it's my recording studio, soundproofed to the max and the only place in the world I want to be.

I made a deal with this indie record label out of California. Nothing major; I'm through with all that success bullshit. Just someone to get my music into the hands of whoever wants to listen. I might sell one copy, I might sell 100,000. Either way I'll be happy.

The pay's shit, but who needs money when you've got cult status? Besides, residuals keep me in CD's and cigarettes.

I'm remixing this bluesy track I've been working on for weeks when I see Stephanie sitting on my couch.

"You look better than you did last time I saw you," she says, and I can tell by the look in her eyes that she's not just blowing smoke up my ass.

"Thanks. You look pretty much the same."

"The curse of long life," she says, smiling, and I realize she's revealed more about her true nature in that sentence than in every other conversation we've ever had.

She pats the couch next to her and I take a seat.

"Thanks," I say.

"For what?"

"Bringing me here."

"It's not something you need to thank me for. It's what I do. Why I was sent here in the first place."

I get the sense that Stephanie is on the brink of spilling all the answers I've been waiting for since I was a kid. Just a little urging and I'll understand Stephanie's reason for being; why she delivers her mixed blessings. Why she chose me. But I understand myself well enough now to know the mystery is what I'm really in love with.

"You just here to check on me, or do you have some nugget of wisdom you've been saving? Maybe a stock tip?"

She laughs. "You're in a good place now."

"The best place. Guess you won't be staying long?"

"I can hang around for a while if you need me to."

I shake my head. "Go change somebody's life."

I realize it's very possible I'm seeing Stephanie for the last time. Before she can disappear, I kiss her, then I ask the one question I can't stand to leave unanswered.

"Do you love me?"

Stephanie shrugs, and that's good enough for me.

ॐ

Liner notes:

Growing up I wanted to be either a rock star or a writer. I honestly didn't care which. I eventually learned that I'm much better at making up stories than I am at playing guitar, but I haven't forgotten those high school garage days, hanging out with friends and making music because there really wasn't anything else to do in a town so small.

Now I just write about music and I live my rock and roll life vicariously through my oldest friend Jay, guitar technician to the stars. The Skid Row mention is for him.

If I'd had enough determination and talent to claw my way out of the garage and pursue an actual career in music, it might have played out something like "Stephanie Shrugs."

But probably not.

Recommended Listening:
Skid Row—*Skid Row*
Nirvana—*Bleach*
The Clash—*The Clash*
The Get Up Kids—*Something to Write Home About*
The New Amsterdams—*Worse for the Wear*

ॐ

Nikola and the Wolf

Nikola stood on the banks of the Hudson and watched the impossible ship approach. The craft was a great galleon with three square-rigged masts and a wooden siren wailing from the bow. But the ship was otherwise unlike those rescued from memory by the likes of Stevenson and Fairbanks. Its masts were great swaying antennas that split the sky behind them with blue streaks of electricity, and its patched sails were singed and trailing smoke. Electricity webbed out in the ship's wake with an eruption of sparks that popped and screamed across the wave crests. They were not yet close enough for Nikola to see the crew, but he knew they must be coming for him.

What remained of the laboratory building burned behind him, discharge coils spilled over like children's blocks, myriad antennas writhing like snakes as they dug into the stones. The air was heavy with ozone, and invisible fingers pulled at Nikola's gray hair. Blue light danced on his fingertips and sizzled when he touched finger to thumb. Overhead, the night sky was torn. As the rip in reality expanded, sparks spilled from the unnatural night like dying stars.

He watched the distant lights of the city flicker on and off, and unable to process the enormity of his folly, Nikola sat where the land met the river and waited for the ship. It drew to a stop and shadowed figures lowered a small boat with a three-man crew into the water. Yellow and red dots bobbed in the darkness around them; they looked to Nikola like men besieged by fireflies. When at last the boat thudded against the rocks, Nikola stood and beheld them.

They were not men, but humanoid machines dressed in high boots, billowing shirts and salt-stained leather belts. Their skin was a silvery metal that Nikola couldn't at once recognize, and their arms were hinged in several places, allowing a range of motion unequalled by humanity. Their legs were similarly appointed, and they approached in short, graceful strides. There was no clanking sound of machinery, and no apparent power source save for the short antennas that each had growing from behind one earhole. Nikola thought vaguely of his dream of wireless power, and wondered if something grand might have grown from his disastrous experiment.

"Impossible," he mumbled. "They are powered with batteries."

The three robots stopped before him. Then with eerie silence they dropped to one set of knees and pressed their heads to the ground. Their machinery seemed unaffected by the water pooling around them, though electrical charges danced along their skin in the same manner it clung to their ship. Nikola's instinct was to fear electrocution, but the electricity slithered across his forearms in a similar fashion and he knew he was in no danger.

Yellow and green lights flicked on and off, aligned on the robots' backs and fronts in a seemingly random pattern. The one in the middle lifted his head and stared at Nikola with lightbulb eyes. They dimmed, and then flared up again as if experiencing a temporary loss of current.

"I'm Short Wave Silver," he said. "And this is me crew. Now you're a god and can do as you wish, but the Wolf Lord requests the blessing of your presence, and he's sent us to deliver you whole to him. Will you come, or must we go to our deaths trying to fulfill the master's wishes?"

Nikola considered the destruction behind him and the madness of the creatures before him. Whatever his experiments had done, they would lead to questions he could not answer, and possibly to prison. The robots seemed relatively harmless, but he was not certain what might be required to defend himself from kidnapping.

"My choices seem rather limited," he said, then stepped into the bobbing boat and waited for his captors to row him to their ship.

x

Aging boards creaked beneath Nikola's shoes while blue light rippled across the deck in a series of hissing waves. He stood immune to the electricity's bite, something more and less than human.

Though ostensibly a prisoner, Nikola stood unbound beside Short Wave Silver as the captain barked orders to his robot crew. Upon his return to the ship, the captain had donned his tricorn hat of office and a parrot had taken perch on his shoulder. The bird sported a brilliant rainbow of plumage, and mimed each of the captain's commands in a high voice that crackled with static.

Wind billowed the smoking sails and the ship moved at a steady clip. Overhead, the hole in the sky continued to expand and began to leak colors. What had he done? He wondered if this whole experience was a Nazi plot. Some way of striking back at the American home front by driving men insane with hallucinations that underlined their own failings. Or worse, perhaps they wanted to use his knowledge for their war effort.

"Are you taking me to Berlin?" asked Nikola.

"Nay," said the Captain, distracted by his duties.

"Then where *are* you taking me?"

"To the Wolf Lord."

"So you say. But who is the Wolf Lord?"

"God of the waves."

"One of the Fuhrer's submarine captains?"

"God of the *radio* waves," said Silver. They'd moved into deep waters and Silver turned over command of the ship to his first mate, a slender assemblage of rusted pipes and loose wires that coughed out huge clouds of smoke with each step. The robot didn't speak, but acknowledged the order with a rapid flash of his eye lights. Silver beckoned Nikola to follow, and they descended a steep staircase and entered the captain's cluttered cabin.

The captain moved a pile of cabling and metal scraps from the room's only chair and offered Nikola a seat. The room hummed as if the moldy wooden walls held at bay raging rivers of electrical current. Nikola was quickly growing accustomed to the sound. Electricity seemed as pervasive as air in this new world he'd inadvertently spawned.

"Thirsty?" asked Silver. He offered a cloudy container half filled with a viscous black liquid. Nikola declined with a wave of his hand and Silver drank greedily. He sat on the edge of his bed and the parrot leaped from his shoulder and lit on Nikola's knee. He could feel the vibration from what he assumed was the bird's internal motor.

"I find that this new world confuses me," said Nikola. He was not speaking to Silver, but the captain rearranged his jaw into the semblance of a grin.

"No more confusing than any other, I'll wager," he said. "The Wolf Lord's as good a master an any."

"And how long have you been in his service."

Silver's eye bulbs dimmed as he considered this. "Always. Since the beginning of things."

"And when was that?"

"Too many centuries to count. But what be time to a god like you?"

Nikola sighed. "I am no god. I am a failure. And I have no idea what your Wolf Lord wants with the likes of me."

"Nor do I, Mr. Tesla. But the Wolf Lord commands and I'm bound to follow. 'Tis the way of things. The Wolf Lord worships you, we metal men worship him, and yet here you be. Our prisoner. It seems none of us have the helm of our own destiny."

Nikola started to ask what the captain meant about the Wolf Lord worshiping him when the humming in the ship's walls turned into a static scream. Sparks hissed from the ceiling and suddenly music was playing. It was unlike any music Nikola had ever heard, a rapid, noisy clatter of instruments that seemed plumbed from the mind of a demon.

Silver dropped to his knees and cocked his antenna skyward. "The Wolf Lord commands!"

The volume of the music increased to the point of pain. A voice careened through the galloping song, screaming "c'mon, c'mon, c'mon" to someone named Little Darling, and when the song became so loud that Nikola felt tears welling in his eyes, it stopped.

His ears whined in the sudden silence. "*That* is the voice of your master?"

"The Wolf Lord speaks to us in song. To hear the growl of his true voice would mean death."

"I do not see how you can determine meaning from such garbled speech."

"The Wolf Lord's demands be obvious, sir. He grows impatient with the progress of this vessel. He commands us to quicken our pace."

x

In the proceeding seconds, hours, days, months on the ship (time was no longer a commodity of any value) Nikola grew accustomed to the Wolf Lord's musical demands. They were like puzzles to be solved, and though he failed often, he grew more adept at divining their intent. The pirates believed that the violent noise accompanying the Wolf Lord's words was an attempt to further encrypt their meaning. Those who were truly intended to hear his messages could do so, and the pirates took this as evidence that they were among the Wolf Lord's chosen few.

One of the Wolf Lord's "psalms" (as the pirates referred to them) revealed that he could see for miles and miles, and Nikola took this to mean that he was aware of their progress toward whatever their destination. Another psalm asked them to love him two times, and Nikola interpreted this to mean the Wolf Lord wanted his servants to prioritize him above all other gods. Other psalms, like the one demanding they get off of his cloud, made no sense at all, and only Short Wave Silver claimed to understand them.

Nikola had determined that the ship was nothing more than a large radio receiver, and likewise the antennae on the robot's heads were smaller versions of the same. He wasn't certain who or what the Wolf Lord might be, but whatever the origin of these transmissions, the pirates took them as gospel truths.

Then one afternoon, beneath one of the Wolf Lord's marmalade skies, Captain Silver called, "Land, ho!" Nikola drew his gaze away from the notebook he'd been scribbling in and spotted a vague line of green curling along the horizon. Blue gashes of electricity screamed skyward from the growing land mass. Soon they were close enough for him to see jungle huddled against the sands, and several large spires poked out from its depths. They were constructed of rough wood and leaves and wound with wire, like giant radio towers erected by primitives. Deep in the jungle, one spire rose higher than all, and Nikola judged it must be the source of the Wolf Lord's spiritual transmissions.

"Gather your things, sir," said Silver.

Nikola had nothing to gather save for the pencil and pad he'd been clutching when his experiments went awry. He flattened his lapels, straightened his jacket and allowed Silver and several of his crew to row him to shore.

"This is where your God lives?" asked Nikola. He did not believe that any sort of god lived here, but he'd learned it was useless to argue with the pirates. They were fanatics.

"Aye," said Silver. "His temple lies in the heart of the jungle."

"Have you seen him then?"

"Nay. To look upon him would dim the eyes."

They reached the beach and disembarked from the boat.

A gang of robot pirates greeted them, most showing deference to Captain Silver. They were engaged in a number of activities associated with storybook piracy: three shoveled a hole while an ornate chest awaited burial; another scribbled a map to the location on yellowed parchment. All held bottles of rum and many wore patches over one shattered eye lamp. Robot innards hung from yardarms, the doomed constructs' silvery shells stripped away by the elements and flocks of glowing birds.

"Who's the prisoner?" asked a heavy set robot with one wooden leg. A nest of wires coiled from his chin to form a beard.

"The object of me quest. A gentleman by the name of Mr. Tesla."

"The Wolf Lord's own god?"

"Aye, Sparkbeard. The one and only."

Sparkbeard scowled. "So, find him ye did? Well, you'll rise in his favor no doubt. Should have been me that found him, but so long as he's delivered then Providence is served, aye?"

"Aye," said Silver, and they shook hands.

"Don't delay then," said Sparkbeard. "I'll take him there if ye require a rest."

"An unnecessary kindness," said Silver, his eyes flaring. He obviously had no wish to share his prize. "I'll take him to the temple me self."

"Then take him before these curs steal him from you and claim the credit."Sparkbeard's tone left no doubt that he would be among said curs if the opportunity arose.

"Shall we be about, Mr. Tesla?" asked Silver.

Nikola nodded and together they entered the jungle.

x

Nikola sweltered in his wool suit. The man he was before the accident could never have imagined such a circumstance: trudging through jungle mud with a robot pirate to answer a summons from a self-styled god of radio. This entire reality was obviously a product of his failures, and he wondered what other nightmares existed in this new world.

He'd wanted nothing more than to prove his critics the fools they were. Certainly Edison was long in his grave, but Nikola had won that particular war. Yet others had arisen to questions his visions, and as his theories had grown more fantastic, so had their mocking protests. But his theories were not fantasies; they shattered the boundaries of known science to be sure, but he believed science should not be a discipline of limitations. Using properties of electricity and magnetism to control space and time would allow men to transfer themselves from one location to another, to travel in anti-gravity machines, to move through time and change every yesterday. What greater boon could mankind receive?

And yet this jungle, this madness, was the price of his arrogance. He had certainly manipulated space and time, but they had rebelled.

"I still do not understand why this god of yours demands an audience with me. Does he think I can fix this? That is impossible. It is done."

"Fix what?" asked Silver as he hacked through a vine with his sword.

"This reality. You must be from the far future. You can only be here because of the damage I've caused."

"We've been here long years before the Wolf Lord even spoke of you. And how many days ago did this *damage* occur? Five? Ten?"

"That matters little," said Nikola. "The limitation of time has been stripped from the universe."

"Yet it's taking a damned long time to hack through this jungle," said Silver. His attempt at humor did not impress Nikola.

"You would not understand anyway," he said. "I'll save my questions for your master."

Silver did not take offence. "Aye, perhaps that's for the best."His sword hissed through a wall of overgrown grass, then the pirate pulled back the dewed green blades like he was parting a curtain. "This is his lair, scientist. I'll go no farther, but you'll tell him it was Short Wave Silver that delivered you to his magnificence. Aye?"

"I will," said Nikola. He bore no malice toward his captor. It was ultimately the Wolf Lord that was responsible for this scenario. And he had to admit, there was a thrilling sense of adventure to it all.

How many men were given the opportunity to explore the ruin of their dreams?

Nikola pushed through the grass and stepped into a massive area of cleared earth surrounded by seemingly impenetrable jungle. At the center of the clearing stood a massive pyramid with stair-step sides. Nikola was not a dedicated historian, but it was obviously a pre-Columbian structure. At the apex of the pyramid was an antenna of more recent construction, a latticework spire of metal and wood with an XERB logo lit up in green fluorescent light. Electricity whispered across its surface and bled out onto the pyramid below. Glowing blue light pooled at its base and ran off like rainwater through rivulets in the earth.

Robots milled about, clearing away patches of encroaching jungle and cooking some sort of skinned animal in a stone fire pit. They were not dressed as pirates; their attire was foreign to Nikola. A few gave him questioning stares, but none bothered to stop him until he reached the base of the pyramid. Two robots stood guard, one heavyset with a pinstriped jacket and a wide smile, the other a slender construction with thick black glasses over a pair of tiny bulb eyes.

"Helllooooo, Baby!" said the heavyset robot. "You here to see the Wolf?"

"I am. My name is Nikola Tesla and I believe your master is expecting me."

"He sure is," said the second robot, head bobbing. "He sent the Martians up in one of them rocket ships yesterday. They told him the boat was headed this way. He's waiting on you-who-who."

Nikola nodded, not sure what to make of the robots. "You are not pirates?"

"Not hardly," said the heavyset robot. "They're a superstitions bunch. You'll never catch them this close to the Wolf."

"I find this world grows stranger by the second."

"It surely does," said the robot. "Normally me and Buddy here would have to get clearance to let you through, but since you're an expected guest, I figure you can head on up to the top."

"My thanks," said Nikola, then he began his ascent.

He was not a young man, and the climb took its toll. He struggled up each step, wondering what this new collection of robots was supposed to represent, and amazed at the prospect of actual Martians. The Wolf's horrible music was pervasive in this place, and Nikola felt weighed down by chants of "baby, baby" and by the thundering drum beats.

When at last he reached the top of the pyramid, he could see the endless roof of the jungle and smell the scent of cooked meat wafting up from the fire pit below. Captain Silver's ship was a distant speck on the beach. Wind whipped at Nikola's hair and he grabbed one of the great radio tower's metallic legs to steady himself. Beneath the tower, a wild-eyed man sat behind a rickety desk. The desk was bare save for a radio transmitter, a record player and a microphone. Odd-sized records surrounded him like vinyl chaos, some in stacks, others spilled over onto the stone pyramid and sliding over the edge. The man grinned at Nikola and motioned him toward a second chair, just outside the sea of records.

"Tesla! The man himself, knock knocking on my door! Drop back in that chair and sit for a while."The Wolf Lord's voice was an animal growl, but for all his claims of godliness he was simply a grinning man with a heavy beard and a barely tamed nest of gleaming black hair. Nikola took his seat.

"You hungry?" asked the Wolf Lord. "I've got Elvis cooking up a jaguar down there."

"No, thank you."

"Hang on," said the Wolf Lord. He lifted a record off the player and tossed it over his shoulder. "You like The Beatles? Oh, man, of course you don't. You don't even know what the hell I'm talking about, do you?" The Wolf Lord dug through the pile of records then finally settled on one and placed it on the player. When he dropped the needle, someone began singing over music and handclaps, and the Wolf Lord howled along with the tune. Nikola sat patiently until the singer began to wail about holding someone's hand and finally he could wait no longer.

"Sir, I must ask why you've brought me here. I think I've been more than patient throughout this ordeal."

The Wolf Lord's eyes snapped open. "Sorry. Songs like that grab me by the throat and drag me somewhere else, you know?"

"I fear I've never had much time for trivial pursuits."

"Well, if that's your way then let's dig deep down to the heart of the matter. You want to know why I had you brought here? Hell if I know." The Wolf Lord gave a throaty laugh. "Part of me wanted to thank you, I guess. But mainly I just want to ask you what the point is."

"The point?"

"The reason I'm here. All the answers about life, the universe, the whole greasy enchilada! Isn't that what men are supposed to ask their gods? How come you put me here with all this crazy ass free will? I mean, thanks and all that, but I'm not sure I understand it."

Nikola sighed. "Then you will be saddened to learn that I have no more understanding of these events than you. You call me a god, but I am no more divine than you."

"Didn't you invent the radio?" asked the Wolf Lord.

"I certainly did! Though others would argue against hard facts."

"Well then you're damn sure my creator. There might be a Bob Smith without radio, but there wouldn't be any Wolfman. What I don't understand is how I got here. It's like I have this destiny that I've already lived, and yet here I am in this place where anything I imagine comes to pass."

"Then it seems more likely that *you're* the god."

"Maybe. But you're the one who made things this way." The man who called himself Wolfman changed records again without pulling his gaze from Nikola.

"It was an accident."

Wolfman grinned. "That's not exactly what you like hearing from your creator."

"Mr. Wolfman—"

"Just call me Jack."

"Very well, Jack. You must understand that I was engaged in a somewhat theoretical field of study and a miscalculation on my part has resulted in what you see here." Nikola waved his arms around to indicate the swirl of madness that surrounded them. As if on cue, the sky once again began raining multicolored sparks. "All times are one, all places are one, and this island is likely a manifestation of what lives in your dreams. I've done detailed research into a phenomenon I call thought photography, a possible extension of the magnetic and electrical properties that drive the universe. You see, if we perceive light as both a particle *and* a wave—"

"Hang on, man," Jack said. "You're talking gibberish. It all sounds like magic to me. But whatever this is, you're overthinking it. You might be some sort of genius, but I've got this figured out better than you."

Nikola stiffened. "Then perhaps you can *explain*."

"Okay. You say the robots, the space ships, all this endless rock and roll comes from me, and I was already pretty sure that was the case. I used to love all those old science fiction magazines growing up; same with pirate stories. And I'm obviously more than a little touched by rock and roll. So this accident of yours puts me here and this craziness just comes spilling out of me."

"I believe I just stated that this all comes from your dreams," said Nikola. "This is hardly new information."

"Yeah, but I'm not the only record in the jukebox, you dig? This ain't all about me. Why can't *your* dreams become reality?"

The wind was warm and Nikola was uncomfortable in his suit. He loosened his collar and wiped the back of his neck with a handkerchief. "My dreams erupted into flames on a cold New York night in nineteen forty-three. Public humiliation and financial ruin will be the payment for my failure."

"But you didn't fail!" Jack started another record and jumped up from his seat. He pounded on the desk and howled. "You did it. You gave us control of everything! And you have the power too. If you don't want to be here, then all you have to do is think about where it is you want to go and you're there. If you're dreaming about flying cars and jetpacks...whatever. It becomes real! You didn't fail. You created honest to God freedom, baby!"

Freedom?

Light and pain erupted in Nikola's head and he found himself howling along with Jack. He'd grown accustomed to these attacks over the years. They always accompanied his greatest epiphanies. And though this one came from Jack and not his own mind, it was no less affecting. Visions flooded his mind, countless souls creating their own destinies, their own realities, each one spiraling off from another into an endless sequence of worlds, none affected by any other, each as real as the next yet all the product of imagination. As the pain receded to a dull thunder in his skull, Nikola pulled his pad and pencil from his jacket and began making furious notes.

"Dear god!" he said. "Do you realize what powers you've given me?"

Wolfman grinned, and he very much resembled his namesake. "Ain't that the way? Gods get what power they have from their worshipers? And besides, you gave the same thing to me. Hell, you gave it to everyone. Once they figure that out, the world's gonna get wild."

Jack reached across his desk and snatched Nikola's pencil from his hand. "Why are you making notes? This ain't about science any more. It's about faith. And it's about fun. Hell, I could have willed you here, but a pirate quest had a lot more pizzazz, you know?"

"It is very much about science, young man!" Nikola pushed back his chair and clapped his hands. "Do you understand what we have here? A multiplicity of universes! And not existing universes, but actual worlds created by my work!" He returned to his writing, thinking about Edison, Einstein, Marconi and all the others who'd sparred with his genius. His perception was now reality. All of his theories were now facts. What would they think if he visited them in their time and faced them down with the evidence of his brilliance?

And then the smell of cooking jaguar and the hot breath of Jack's island wind were at once replaced with a frigid, snowbound New York street. Nikola knocked at a familiar door as horse-drawn carriages clattered past behind him. The world had a scent it had not had in many years; the tinge of stove smoke mingled with animal musk. Nikola recognized this place, this time. And when Thomas Edison opened the door, he was the pleasant man Nikola had first met so many years ago, and not the bitter rival their relationship had cultivated.

"May I help you, sir?" asked Edison.

"My name is Nikola Tesla, and you will meet me soon."

"I'm meeting you now, sir," said Edison. He seemed puzzled but not unfriendly.

"Indeed. Here, I have something for you." Nikola's whim conjured a sheaf of scientific papers. He handed the bound collection to Edison and noticed his own hand had scrawled *Proven Theories of the Tesla Multiverse* across the outer page. "I think you will find these papers illuminating."

"What is this about?" asked Edison.

"This is about a new way of viewing the world," said Nikola. "No longer is mankind bound by the laws of physics. Now he can write them himself."

"Why are you bringing this to me?"

"So that when you read them, you will understand who is the true genius," said Nikola with a slight smile.

Then he left Edison standing in the doorway and turned his mind to other worlds.

CB

Liner notes:
This is what happens when you sit out the World Fantasy Awards in favor of watching Longhorn football and chatting with friends. This was in the middle of the Great Pirate Story Push of 2006 and several of us hadn't written our obligatory offerings yet. We began tossing out ideas (we being, as I recall, my wife Kristin, Mikal Trimm, Sam Henderson, and Eric Marin, though memory is a shaky thing) and all I knew for certain was that I wanted to make my pirate story a pirate *radio* story.

Thinking about radio led me to Tesla and to Wolfman Jack, and by the time I put the whole thing together, I realized that the actual pirates in the story had been relegated to bit players. By the next day, the story was all but assembled in my head, but I let it stew for a while and eventually had the thing written in time to hit the pirate anthology slush. Ultimately the story wasn't about pirate radio at all, but it did have pirates.

As I'd feared, the story was well received but wasn't "piratey" enough to make the cut anywhere. So here for the first time is my one and only pirate story.

Sort of.

Recommended Listening:
Soundtrack—*American Graffiti*
Buddy Holly—*From the Original Master Tapes*
The Beatles—*With the Beatles*

CB

Bury My Guitar at Wounded Knee

November 21, 1855

Letter from Jonathan Crowe to his wife, Clara Crowe

My Dearest Clara,

By the Grace of Providence I have reached my destination. This is a bitterly cold place, and the relentless wind is an ever present reminder of the warmth of hearth and family I have left behind in Atlanta. It is evident to me why Jackson chose this land for the Indians' exile. None other would want it. Food is scarce unless you are industrious enough to trap prairie chickens or some breed of vermin, and the water is the same color as the soil. We are without even the meanest of urban facilities and the buildings, poorly constructed wooden hovels, barely serve as adequate windbreaks, let alone shelters from the snow that threatens.

This is what we have left for these people. You know my feelings on this sad state of affairs, my lovely Clara, and this added ignominy is but fuel for my resolve. I will find the man I seek and discover what I may about the true nature of those our Great American Progress has banished from our civilized lands.

I shall write as often as possible, and pray that my posts will reach you. All my love to you and the children.

Yr. Husband & Servant,

Jonathan

os

December 1, 1855

Letter from Jonathan Crowe to his wife, Clara Crowe

My Dearest Clara,

A stroke of luck! After a week of fruitless searching, I have met a man, a Mr. Sam Phillips late of Memphis, Tennessee and apparent friend and trading partner of the very band of Indians I seek. Surely this is a sign that God smiles on my work! Truth be told, Phillips does not seem a man to be overly trusted, and is given to braggadocio. But others corroborate his claims and I believe he will lead me to Blue Shoes and his company if given financial incentive.

Mr. Philips assures me their camp is not far to the west, and if this is the case, then I shall be home sooner than expected. I must finish writing and gather my belongings. We leave in the morning by horseback. Tell Eleanor and little Lizzy that their father will return soon with presents and hugs, and perhaps a story that will ensure our financial futures.

Yr. Servant,

Jonathan

os

January 20, 1856

Letter from Jonathan Crowe to his wife, Clara Crowe

Clara my Love,

All apologies for the length of time between letters, but the matter could not be helped. I pray you have not fretted overmuch for my safety. I have just returned to some measure of civilization after weeks on the plains. I thought of you all on Christmas and I greatly regret having missed the sight of our precious little girls on that blessed morning.

Mr. Phillips was half as good as his purchased word. The promised horses were in fact mules, and hardly the zenith of their sorry species, so travel to Blue Shoes' encampment took all of three weeks. I will spare you the discomfort of that journey, but suffice it to say that I have gladly eaten creatures that I would not serve dogs in Atlanta and my throat was a desert for lack of clean water. For a time there were modest hills and thickets of trees to break the cold, but eventually they gave way to the endless, hellish plains that no man should have to tread upon, much less call home. This is a new sort of wilderness to me, one of stark emptiness, where even the wild grasses could not aspire to the height of my boot straps and the few stunted trees were too busy fighting for their own existence to provide any coverage from the wailing winds. Never have I been more delighted to spot red firelight than I was when Blue Shoes' village came into sight. I feared that we would be turned away, a pair of white men helpless and begging, but Blue Shoes and his men were among the most companionable of hosts that I could have wished.

You should see the man, Clara! He is everything the rumors make of him and more. His people were originally of Mississippi, but as a boy he trod the westward path of Jackson's decree, and saw his father and mother laid low by the pox and starvation. His twin brother was bitten by a snake while crossing the Arkansas River and joined them in death. Still, he is a jovial Cherokee, if a little eccentric. He slicks his thick hair with buffalo fat and styles it high with a lazy curl stuck fast to his forehead. His eyes are a piercing blue that captivates the young women of the renegade tribe, and he further elicits their admiration with a frenetic dance that involves a wildly improper shaking of his hips. And the songs he sings! They are howling, urgent entreaties to the night, as if he cries worship to one of his pagan gods, and I have never heard their like.

Blue Shoes surrounds himself with like minded individuals, and they share his love for dancing and ungodly music. Chief among them is a constantly smiling Creek whose name translates to The Killer. It is easy to spot the spark of madness in his eyes, and his smile takes on a more sinister quality because of it. Another of the men names himself John Cash after a white man who tried to pistol whip him in Illinois. He would not speak of the attacker's fate, but I suspect he stole the man's life as well as his name.

Curiously, one of Blue Shoes' closest confidants is not an Indian at all, but a white man. He is a wiry, hardened youth that they call Perkins. He speaks little and had not volunteered any other name. They are the obvious leaders of the tribe and often join Blue Shoes in his nightly dancing and singing. When they combine their talents in this sort of racket, the result is almost too much to bear. Others blow on curiously carved flutes and beat sticks against stretched animal hides, and the music is nothing short of a dangerous intoxicant. I am loath to admit that I found myself swaying to the pagan rhythms on more than one icy evening. Blue Shoes himself plays a strange handmade guitar, and he does so standing; the instrument hangs from his neck and shoulders by a rope.

This tribe is unlike any other in my readings, being comprised of any number of races of Indian, without regard for their Nations.

Though Comanche and Kiowa may battle on the wide southern planes, they sing and hunt together under Blue Shoes' rule, and not once in my weeks with them did I witness any ire between man and man. All are welcomed—Indians, outlaws and escaped slaves—so long as they adhere to the spirit of the camp, and so long as they are willing to participate in the nightly songs. It is a savage utopia they've created in their forcibly adopted homeland, and they have made far more of their exile than anyone could have imagined.

Blue Shoes laughed to learn that his tribe has been written of in the Eastern papers, and was further amused to hear that it is my intention to write a novel of his exploits. I assured him that though I may profit (and indeed, it is my sincere hope the profits will be grand) my main desire is to illuminate the nobility of the red man and cast a disapproving pall over the actions of those who would scour the earth of their race.

I offered the man a share of the profits, but he declined. He cares for nothing but his new family and his music, and so long as he is free to live as such, he has no interest in revenge against the nation and the people that drove his family to death. His skirmishes against our forces are only in defense of what is left to him.

Clara, I beg your patience but I must return to the camp. I have written twenty good pages and only returned to town in order to mail them to my prospective publisher in hope of securing funds to further my efforts. I regret again that this task takes me so far from the people I find dearest in the world, but you must agree that helping these people find equality through pen or sword is paramount, and certainly our lives will be improved by the steady income provided by the eventual sale of my epic. I shall write again as soon as humanly possible. All of my love to you and the children.

Your faithful husband,

Jonathan

☙

May 1, 1856

Letter from Jonathan Crowe to Mr. Benjamin Wenner, Publisher

Mr. Wenner,

I hope this latest missive finds you well. You will recall my letter some months back in which I enclosed twenty pages from my novel in progress that details the exile and ultimate redemption of the Cherokee man, Blue Shoes, and his tribe. You will recall, no doubt, certain articles in many of the leading Eastern papers last summer about this man and his rebellion against other tribes and wandering Texas Ranger troops that encroached upon his small claim of land. Refraining from violence, the Sun Tribe as they call themselves simply drove them away with the power of their music.

It sounds utterly absurd, yet I've verified this with more than a few witnesses and furthermore have experienced the eerie charm of their music myself. I hesitate to use the word magic, but as you know it has often been speculated that many of the native peoples have access to un-Christian sources of power. Having felt the utterly surreal call of this unique form of music, I must admit that there is something more to it than our own parlor waltzes.

I received no reply from my last letter, or perhaps your response fell victim to the unreliable nature of letter delivery in this region. Regardless, I feel that these new chapters will convince you that this is a novel project worthy of your company's considerable reputation.

In the event that your time is too valuable to read this entire enclosed segment of the manuscript, I submit the following gripping episode for your consideration. I have done my best to adhere to the truth of the situation, though as this is a work of fiction you will find portions of the narrative embellished for the sake of entertainment, and many of the Indian words replaced with those more intelligible to the educated reader of English:

"You are but a hound dog!" wailed Blue Shoes, calling down lightening with the mere power of his voice. In the distant night, trees burned with unholy fire. Perkins and The Killer moaned in harmony and clanked bits of broken glass against one another. John Cash played the old guitar the tribe shared, creating a tuneless, driving rhythm not unlike the sound of cloven hooves marching free from Hell.

Circling around them, women wailed their pain, pleading to their red god to save their dying way of life. Tears streaked sand-scoured faces, and thunder rumbled overhead as if in answer to their collective cry. The skies opened, and their god bathed them in a shower of tears.

The song changed. "Since my family left," wailed Blue Shoes, "we've found new home in which to dwell. Down at the end of the lonely trail, a heartbroken hell."

The tribe drew more power to it with every word, with every slap of the drum, with every keening wail.

And in the roiling heavens, their god joined the song.

I should be able to complete this thrilling work of fiction and have it entirely delivered to your office within three months. I should think fifty dollars would be adequate to fund the remainder of my research. If you see fit to enter into a mutually beneficial publishing agreement, please demonstrate your good will with the forwarding of these funds and we can discuss the further terms of our agreement at a later date.

Awaiting your imminent response,

Jonathan Crowe

⁓

August 13, 1860

Letter from Jonathan Crowe to Mr. Angus Fillmore

Angus,

Your letter and news from the East was greatly appreciated. Clara no longer answers all of my letters, and has grown increasingly distant. She has made no secret of her desire for my immediate return, and those brief messages that she posts state as much. But she refuses to understand the importance of my travels. She feels I am abandoning my family, yet every dollar I can spare finds its way to Clara and the girls. The payments for my newspaper articles are not generous, but once I find a book publisher for these astonishing tales, we shall all be very wealthy.

In response to your question, the events detailed in my last article were in fact true and not in any sense exaggerations. The Indian music created by Blue Shoes and his cohorts has spread like contagious madness through the plains, and if rumors are to be believed, even to the northern territories. But you misunderstand about Blue Shoes' intentions. It was never his desire to use the music against anyone, but once he tapped such power, he gained with it an unshakable responsibility.

He did not so much teach it to the other tribes as invite them into his soul. They came to hear his music and took it from him. With such power at their command, many tribes see it as a way to rebel against the endless pressure on all sides from the whites. Treaties have been made and land granted, all documented and signed by our own government and yet these legalities are worth less than nothing to the United States. For the most part, the Indians uphold their ends of these agreements, even when it means leaving their ancestral lands. Tell me then, if we are supposed to be the superior, more honorable race, why we do not honor our promises as the Indians do?

Please do not think me some kind of rebel. I am loyal to my country even when I question her motives. I pray every day that she remains sound, and that rumors of a coming conflict will not prove true. Many of the Indians I speak with look forward to such a war. They believe that if the Great Father (as they call our noble president) and his troops are engaged in battle with one another, their presence in the west will be lessened. It is certainly possible, though I am losing faith that anything can save these people from total banishment.

You have read my article about the three great Comanche war chiefs who met their end at the hands of Texan forces last December. I was not present for the battle, but I have heard such vivid descriptions of how burning cold that night was, and how fiercely the chiefs and the people fought back with their music. The greatest of them was Wide Eyes (so called by his people because of the heavy pair of glasses he always wore, scavenged from a fallen Texan in some unknown conflict) yet even his potent music could not prevail against the encroaching Rangers. Though the three chiefs called down lighting and shook the earth with their songs, each of them ended up slain by simple bullets, their battle lost, their people routed.

What use is such great power if it is not enough to prevail against what seems to be inevitable destruction? There is a quiet sadness in the remaining Comanche tribes, and even as they choose new chiefs to lead them in war, they have taken to calling this awful battle "The Day the Music Died." They have lost faith in their own power, and I am sickened that many of these noble men have already chosen defeat as their final fate.

I know that you may find it difficult to sympathize with these people who are portrayed as little more than savages to the vast majority of the public, but you must understand they are no less men than we are. For this reason, I must remain in the west. I am a single voice, but one is a start. You are my great friend, Angus, and I beg that you continue to call on my family and look to their well being while I am away. Take my love to Clara and the children, and to your own lovely Imogene.

Yr. Loyal Friend,
Jonathan Crowe

ೞ

May 15, 1861

Western Union telegram from Jonathan Crowe to his wife, Clara Crowe

Clara,

War is here. Hate me if you will, but take children to your family in Boston. We are no part of this. Safety is paramount. My eternal love to you and the girls.

Jonathan

⊗

June 6, 1862

Letter from Jonathan Crowe to Mr. Angus Fillmore

Angus,

Your letter reaches me in good health. I have indeed left Blue Shoes' tribe to wander north. This music continues to spread and I find my fascination for its power will no longer allow me to remain in place. Blue Shoes gifted me with one of his aging guitars, a token of friendship upon my departure, and that alone seems to have allowed me safe passage through the lands of the Cheyenne and Arapaho, and here into the Dakota country. This is not to say they are violent people, but that they fear the treachery of the white man and if not for Blue Shoes' talisman, I could have found myself victim of a revenge minded young Indian. I have found the elders sue for peace while the young thirst for revenge. I pray wisdom shall prevail.

I have been introduced to musicians of neighboring Sioux tribes who have banded their strength together in one defiant voice. They are Ring Fingers, Nowhere Man, Weeping Guitar and Man-of-Yesterday-Song. Together they make music with a passion surpassing even that of Blue Shoes and his collective, and the magic their god rewards them with is abundant. Their influence on neighboring tribes cannot be understated, and those who can use this music to their advantage are proliferating throughout the west.

Many of the northern tribes have taken to calling these war musicians *rockers*, though I do not know if the term originates in the way they sway too and fro during their ululations or from the way they strike stones together in the wild abandon of their poetic prayers. Regardless, they are everywhere, and though few wish to use their music for war, they have been left little choice.

I am sorry that your injury keeps you from the lines, as I know you are quite eager to fight for your homeland, just as these Indians are, and I appreciate your call to join my "Confederate Brothers" but you must understand that I can claim no allegiance to either side of this conflict. I am a Georgia man, but I cannot countenance the subjugation of the black slave any more than I can that of the red Indian. I likewise have no allegiance to the Bluecoats because I have seen what their ways have wrought in these lands. I am white, so I am able to send and receive letters from the fort, and the soliders will even spare food and conversation. But they regard the Sioux as animals, and would turn me away or imprison me if I made it known that I am a friend of the People.

I pray for your safety in these horrible times, and for that of my family. I appreciate the continued care and attention you pay to them, and would ask you once again to speak with Clara about moving from Atlanta. She pays me no heed, but she may yet listen to you. She needs to be with family that can protect her now. I am a failure as a husband and father, but that does not mean I do not fear for their welfare.

Praying for an end to this all,

Jonathan Crowe

CB

September 10, 1864

Western Union telegram from Jonathan Crowe to Angus Fillmore

Have received your tidings. My despair is boundless. What kind of monsters are these men who would burn women and children? Seek safety where you must. This atrocity shall be avenged.

CB

December 25, 1864

Letter from Jonathan White Crow to Angus Fillmore

Angus,

Merry Christmas, my friend. I have no idea if this letter will reach you, or indeed if you are still alive. I know that after the burning of Atlanta you fled with your family to Savannah, and now I learn that the Devil Sherman has marched a trail of blood and fear that has carried him to the coast. Peace be with your soul, living or dead.

I will never return to the east, for what awaits me but dead and dying memories? Union fires have swallowed my family, my city and my life.

The Indians tell stories of the Thunderbird, an enormous bird that causes thunderclaps with the beating of its wings and issues lighting from its eyes, and some believe it is the power of the Thunderbird that the rockers call upon. It is the personification of violence and destruction, and yet it is universally believed that great happiness lies in the wake of these storms, just as it will lie in the wake of this war of fools and this war against the Indians. There is a glorious peace to strive for, but first there is a hated enemy upon which the power of the Thunderbird must be loosed.

I have no ties left to the places or the people of my country, and will forever make my home as an Indian. I will fight for these people who have made me friend and family. I can not believe in any Southern cause, and I can never side with a Union that would so wantonly lay waste to innocent life.

I am no longer an American. I am a Thunderbird.

Yr. friend always,

Jonathan White Crow

∓

June 18, 1867

Letter from Jonathan White Crowe to Benjamin Wenner

Mr. Wenner,

I am surprised your letter has found me, and I am surprised you chose to write me at all. Your lack of response to my previous missives left me to understand you had little interest in my person or my writing.

Once your offer of publication would have been welcomed news, but the world has changed and it is no longer an offer I can accept. Allow me to be blunt, sir. I can no longer entertain the notion of publishing my fictions as I believe it is no longer possible to convince my fellow Americans that Indians are heroes, and I will not portray them in any other fashion. Likewise, the public will not wish to read of the true deeds committed by its prideful and war polished soldiers.

They will not wish to read of the broken promises and foul mistreatment meted out to the red man at every opportunity. They will not wish to read about the inhuman living conditions that the Navaho were forced to endure at the prison reservation of Bosque Redondo. And I am quite confident they will not be interested to read my descriptions of the Sand Creek massacre, where Bluecoats slaughtered and mutilated not only war chiefs, warriors and rockers, but women and children while their victims pleaded for peace, waving the American flag that was supposed to ensure the safety of all peaceful Arapahos and Cheyenne north of the Platte.

I have no use for your world any more, Mr. Wenner. I am of the People. And though many still urge peace with the white man, I have a keen understanding of how impossible that is.

I am not alone in my outrage. This very day we gather, Sioux, Cheyenne, Arapaho, and we sing out to the Great Spirit, a host of rockers calling for power, calling for vengeance. I lend my guitar to the cause, the guitar that once belonged to the great Cherokee Blue Shoes, and I assure you that if you witnessed the power inherent in this massive concert of discontent, you would not feel safe even those many hundred miles away from the Powder River country.

Red Cloud has worked his people into a war frenzy, and he commands some of the most powerful rockers I've yet encountered.

Purple Cloud is his protégé, a fearsome man always dressed for war in a bonnet of feathers who calls on the Thunderbird with nothing more than the pure fury of his guitar playing. When he wages war with this power, the very world sinks into a soft haze and takes on a disorienting, sinister quality that quite unnerves the Bluecoats. He is joined in song by Rising Sun House, Young-Man-Who-is-Happy-to-be-Dead, the members of the Buffalo Spring Oglala, and other rockers beyond count who make musical prayers together. They enhance their communion with the Great Spirit using the vision inducing drugs of their grandfathers, and in so doing have created the most potent form of war music yet. They are chiefly responsible for the successes so far in Red Cloud's campaign against the Bluecoats who would take what small patch of land remains to us. I am but one voice in these grand preparations, but my heart and soul are committed to victory.

Regrettably yours,

Jonathan White Crow

ᆼ

July 15, 1875

Letter from Jonathan White Crow to Angus Fillmore

Angus,

You are alive! I cannot describe my joy in receiving your letter after so many years have passed. I had lost track of your whereabouts and I have been constantly on the move. Only fortune led me to the old post office, and what happy news to learn that Mr. Wolfman had a letter for me! I am pleased to learn that you and your family are well, and have managed to build such a wonderful new life in North Carolina.

Yes, I am still an avowed expatriate of the United States and you may be shocked to learn that I have even taken up arms against white soldiers. I have killed over thirty of them in various conflicts throughout the northern and southern plains, though always in service of a righteous cause. You have ever been an intelligent, philosophical man, so I pray that you have been able to rationally consider and divine a true understanding of the nation's abhorrent policy of Manifest Destiny. For want of gold and land and righteous superiority, the Americans are reaping souls. What other path remains to the red man but to strike back with similar fury?

I fought alongside Red Cloud and his rockers to save what remained of their hunting lands in the Powder River country and watched as Fort C.E. Smith burned, then Fort Kearney, then Fort Reno. The white men retreated, and the Indians were ceded what was theirs to begin with. Yet when I longed once again to visit the southern plains, I found that the displaced Arapaho and Cheyenne people were still besieged by Bluecoats, even though they had not strayed from the lands they'd been assigned by the Great Father in Washington. Black Kettle's attempts to live in peace resulted in the massacre of his people by Custer's Seventh Cavalry. And even those chiefs who refuse to sign away the slivers of land they have remaining are losing their battles, and worse, losing some of the most powerful rockers aligned with their cause.

It is no secret that if not for the power of the rockers, the People would have been swept from the plains long ago, but as long as the music is alive in this country, there is cause for hope. You have no doubt read about their exploits in the newspapers, and I take some small consolation in the fact that this power that I was once scoffed at for believing in is now documented fact. Yet I feel certain that printed accounts of the Thunderbird power cannot do it justice. Until you have seen the Lizard King light cannons afire with his voice, until you have seen Purple Cloud put a regiment into stupor with windstorms of color and wailing screams, until you have seen Midnight Rider stop bullets with lighting bolts, you have no true understanding of this music's power. Yet all of these great war musicians have lost their lives to Bluecoat bullets, and the solders flow across grass and river and mountain like so many locusts, chewing and destroying everything in their path. I fear their sheer numbers will eventually prove the deciding factor in this unjust campaign of extinction.

Still, there is some cause for hope. When rockers fall, others rise to take their place. I had occasion to meet my old friend Blue Shoes, and though he is not as formidable as he once was, his influence on the younger generation of war musicians cannot adequately be measured. He told me of a traveling band of rockers who will lend their talents to any tribe's cause. They cover their faces in fearsome war paint, and one they call the Demon is reputed to breathe fire. I would discount this claim as utter foolishness had I not witnessed so many other wonders wrought by the music. They wear stacked boots and fearsome suits formed of skins and antlers, and their appearance is said to terrify the whites.

If only these powerful men had been available for Quanah Parker and his Comanche, then perhaps the failure of Adobe Walls, those many battles, and their subsequent surrender would have turned out differently. They are on reservations now, and with them John Cash and The Killer, once formidable rockers and allies of Blue Shoes. He mourns their virtual imprisonment, and prays that this new breed of rocker can succeed where they have failed.

I will soon leave for the north again. The Black Hills call and I once again wish to ride and hunt with my old friends. I will write again, and I pray that you keep in touch. May you and your family continue to prosper.

Yr. Great Friend,

Jonathan White Crow

CB

July 21, 1876

Letter from Jonathan White Crow to Angus Fillmore

Angus,

I have survived a supremely vicious battle. As you have no doubt read, some weeks ago we clashed with Bluecoat solders near the Little Big Horn River. You are surely the only white man concerned with my whereabouts, and though I am pressed for time, I am compelled to write and assure you of my safety.

Crazy Horse has recruited a new breed of rocker to his cause, able to bring the magic to bear in violent, hand to hand combat, whirling and thrashing through startled knots of soldiers with blades of lighting. Their music is louder and less sentimental than any I've heard before, and it contains a primal urgency that seems well suited to the times. One of these men, Rotten John, slew the hated Bluecoat commander Custer in the very midst of his men and emerged from battle unscathed. I have never seen such reckless bravery, and I predict a horrible end for any soldiers foolish enough to mass against these war magicians they've taken to calling punks.

More troops are coming and we must ride. Take care, my friend, and remember us all in your prayers.

Yr. Friend,

Jonathan White Crow

ᙟ

October 22, 1877

Telegram from Jonathan White Crow to Angus Fillmore

I have just received word of Blue Shoes' death two months ago. I take solace that he gave up his soul to the Great Spirit a free man, and not imprisoned on a reservation. I will play him a song tonight on this old guitar, and recall better days.

ᙟ

August 1, 1886

Letter from Jonathan White Crow to Angus Fillmore

Angus,

I ride with Geronimo! We are outlaws from both the American and Mexican governments, and never in my life have I felt such an exhilarating sense of freedom! How I wish that you had one month away from your home and *civilized* responsibilities so that you could experience the smell of battle, and all the visceral joys of truly living. I admit that my age pains me at time, particularly when riding without stop for hours on end, but there are few left these days to fight for what is right, and I will be among them until I am dead.

We are pursued by thousands of soldiers, and yet we number less than two score. They will never find us unless we allow it, and if they do, they will have Geronimo's rockers to contend with. They are a vastly more independent sort than most of the war musicians I have known before, preferring an autonomous joining with the Great Spirit rather than following commands given by any chief. They are loyal to Geronimo, but they will not have him directing their songs. As a result, there is a greater vitality to the music than much of what has gone before.

It can only be by virtue of this magic that we've eluded capture this long. Young Dragon and Noisy Child are brilliant rockers, and their spells are potent weapons against the white men. Blue Shoes would be pleased to see what his simple communion with the gods has evolved into.

I do not know if I will be able to mail this letter, but writing it makes me feel like there is still one connection to the life I left behind long ago. I do not regret my choices in life, but there will always be some part of me that remembers the world I've abandoned with a measure of fondness.

Death or Glory,

Jonathan White Crow

಄

April 4, 1894

Letter from Jonathan White Crow to Angus Fillmore

Angus,

Years have passed since I last wrote, and I must beg your forgiveness. I have spent nearly six years in a Florida prison under conditions of hard labor. I would have attempted to contact you, but I knew you would feel compelled to visit me and I did not want you to see the tired, defeated man I have become. We are both old men now, Angus, but the world has taken far more from me.

I surrendered, with Geronimo, to wily General Miles, after a grand chase. With all of our rockers killed, and little chance of escape, we had few options. They promised Geronimo that there would be a place for his Apaches in Arizona after a brief exile in Florida, but I need not remind you the value of Bluecoat promises. This was in 1887 and we have spent the intervening years, as I described, in prison.

Now free, I have followed Geronimo to Fort Sill in the Oklahoma territory, and we are expected to wither and die like good Indians, and to never cause another moment's trouble. Sadly, few seem to mind it anymore. While I was imprisoned, the People's spirit was finally snuffed out like the tenuous flame it had become. Before our people came to these shores, it was a bonfire. What have we done? Are there any Indians left not confined to the places we put them? They have all been chased from the plains, and even the mighty Sioux, who I thought might truly hold their shrinking portion of the world against the encroaching hordes, have been herded into captivity or simply slaughtered en masse as were those at Wounded Knee.

Perhaps worst of all, the rockers have gone. Certainly there are still those that make music, and cry out to the Great Spirit to infuse them with the power to strike back at their enemies and to change the world. But the connection between man and spirit seems to have been severed. This more than anything demonstrates to me that this battle is over. If you are looking to find just how much has been taken from these people, you need only peer into Geronimo's eyes or watch as he sells his trinkets and memories to settlers. I can no longer bear it.

I must apologize that my only letter to you in these so many years is filled with grief and bitterness, but I wanted to let you know that I am still alive and that there is at least a spark of hope left inside me. I entertain no notion that the People can ever regain what is lost, but there are rumors of one last rocker in this new world, a man wandering the west, and I would track him down and hear another of the holy songs before I die. He is called The Seattle Kid, a name that sounds more like a dime novel gunfighter than a war musician, but the few men I've spoken with that have met him claim that his music is worthy, and he can command the Thunderbird.

I will seek this man. It is likely a fruitless task, but what else is left to me beyond the chasing of memories and dreams?

Yr. Great Friend,

Jonathan White Crow

03

July 19, 1894,

Western Union telegram from Jonathan White Crow to Angus Fillmore

The Seattle Kid is dead. He took his life in despair even before I began my search.

You will not hear from me again, Angus. My adventures have come to an end and I will not burden you with my sorrow any longer. I will play my guitar and hope the Great Spirit finds something pleasing in my songs and comes for me, as He has for so many others.

Those songs and those people will remain in my memory forever. And when I die, we shall all meet again in the Spirit World.

Imagine, Angus, what wonderful music they must have in that place. Death is indeed something to hope for.

ଔ

Liner notes:

European settlers began removing the Native American people from their lands the moment Columbus reached the New World and famously wrote, "I could conquer the whole of them with fifty men, and govern them as I pleased." But the eighteen fifties to the eighteen nineties were among the most contentious decades in United States history and saw the virtual extermination of every tribe that still held to their traditions and homes. A seemingly endless succession of betrayals and indignities left the Native Americans little recourse but to defend themselves against the encroaching settlers and battles raged from the Mississippi to the Pacific Ocean. A detailed account of this period can be found in Dee Brown's excellent history, "Bury My Heart at Wounded Knee."

Fast forward one hundred years and you encounter the rise and fall of rock and roll, an admittedly subjective period of time running from the nineteen-fifties to the early nineteen nineties. I'm not saying no good rock and roll has been made since the nineties. That's hardly the case. But there seems to be a line of demarcation between the way rock and roll <u>was</u> and the way that it is *now*.

I'm not simply talking about commercial aspects of the music—that's always been part of the equation. And I don't think this is simple nostalgia at work. I dig plenty of new rock acts. But rock and roll no longer seems to be the generational mirror and the conduit for self-identification that I've always found it to be. There are exceptions of course, but for the most part modern music is just that. It doesn't define us, it doesn't ask many questions or offer any answers. And worst of all, it doesn't foster an old-fashioned sense of rebellion. It's now something to buy for .99 cents a pop from iTunes so you'll have something to listen to while waiting in line at the mall food court.

Rock and roll is not *important* to people anymore, and this may be more our fault than the music's.

I might be wildly off base, and please take me to task if I am. Show me how modern rock is as relevant as it was in the sixties, the seventies, even the eighties. But from my vantage, we seem to be feasting on rock's corpse as opposed to figuring out how to bring it back to life.

So, eighteen fifties to eighteen nineties...nineteen fifties to nineteen nineties. That's all it takes to get me obsessing over a story, and this is what resulted. I was hoping the music would prove to be the People's savior, but the story went where it wanted, and the ending proved to be inevitable.

Recommended Listening:
Elvis Presley—*Elvis Presley*
The Grateful Dead—*American Beauty*
Jimi Hendrix—*Electric Ladyland*
Sex Pistols—*Never Mind the Bollocks Here's the Sex Pistols*
Dinosaur Jr.—*Ear-Bleeding Country*
Mother Love Bone—*Apple*

Grievous Angel

Farther along we'll know all about it,
Farther along we'll understand why.
Cheer up my brother, come sing in the sunshine,
We'll understand it all by and by
—Traditional

 C8

Before Jeff could leave California for good, he had to visit Gram just one more time.

His old Chevy Cavalier coughed out clouds of gray smoke that seemed to hang forever in the thick, sunny air of Joshua Tree National Park. The Cap Rock loomed ahead, fading sunlight burning red against its surface, giving the rock formation the appearance of a giant bonfire rising above the cholla cactus and the scattering jackrabbits.

"That's it," said Jeff, pointing.

Kate acknowledged his statement with a slow nod that might easily have been a mirage. The air conditioner blasted her blonde hair against the passenger seat headrest. Sunglasses masked her eyes, but her chin trembled just enough to reveal the way she felt about the whole situation.

"How long's this gonna take?" she asked.

"This isn't something I can rush through, okay? You didn't have to come."

"What else was I supposed to do?" she asked, unable to conceal the bitterness in her voice.

"I'm not making you move to Vegas," he said. "You could have stayed in L.A. You can still come with me to Lubbock."

"Some choice. A life alone in L.A. or mooching off my sister in Vegas. It could be worse, I guess. At least you're giving me a ride."

Jeff stopped the car near the base of the Cap Rock. "I told you I'm sorry. I love you, Kate."

"Let's just get this over with. I can't believe we have to stop so you can say goodbye to some dead rock star." She opened the car door, stepped into the dusky twilight and slammed it behind her.

Jeff remained behind the wheel, listening to the engine tick and wondering again if he'd made the right decision.

He figured he might spend the rest of his life wondering that exact same thing.

CR

Jeff's guitar was in the back seat and so was the duffel bag full of tape reels. They were wedged in with the rest of their belongings—suitcases, wrinkled clothes, stacks of CDs and tapes. Jeff removed the guitar and the duffel bag and carried them both to the base of the Cap Rock.

Kate was already there. She stood with her hands shoved in the pockets of her white cotton shorts, bathed in long gray shadows. Wind pulled at her sleeveless green blouse, and watching her made

Jeff's heart ache. He had to remind himself their relationship was coming to an end.

Kate stared across the craggy expanse of rock and brush, not offering so much as a frown of acknowledgement. Still, Jeff felt self-conscious having her with him. He always came to visit this place alone. As stupid as it might sound to some, this was an intensely personal experience. He loved Kate, but this was his way of connecting with the universe. He didn't need an audience.

"You gonna watch from there?" he asked, setting the guitar case and duffel bag at his feet.

"You expect me to wait in the car or something?"

"No," said Jeff, even though that's exactly what he'd expected. But things were strained enough between them; no reason to make it worse by asking her to take a walk.

"Then get on with it," she said.

"Please don't be like this."

"Don't start again, okay?" Kate took a seat on the ground and pulled her knees up against her chest. "Just do what you have to do so we can get the hell out of here."

Jeff opened the guitar case. The familiar scent of aged wood and roadhouse smoke pushed aside the hot medley of desert aromas. He removed the Gibson Dove and strummed a chord. Perfect. It was a damned good guitar, nearly as old as Jeff, and it always seemed to stay in tune. He played a quick chord progression and somewhere in the distance, a quail answered. This had to be the loneliest place on earth. Jeff fit right in.

He took a quarter from his pocket and began playing a faithful rendition of "Streets of Baltimore" from Gram Parson's first solo album. Jeff's voice was warm and world weary, maybe a little more so than it had been in the past, but he could never match the sense of aching loneliness that Gram projected. He'd been trying most of his life, and finally settled for second best.

"I like that song," Kate said when he'd finished. Either the song had calmed her or she'd temporarily run out of anger. She sounded tired. Defeated.

"I know."

"So that's what you do out here? You just play your guitar for Gram Parsons?"

"Yeah, that's about it."

"Why here?"

"This is where his road manager set him on fire."

"Jesus! I thought he died of a drug overdose."

"He did. In a hotel not far from here. Thing is, he and Phil Kaufman—that was his road manager—they made a deal. Which ever one died first, the other would make sure his ashes got spread all over the Joshua Tree desert. From what I've read, Gram spent a lot of time here near the end, writing songs, finding himself. He was buddies with Keith Richards and they used to kick around here all the time. The Cap Rock was his favorite place."

"So this Kaufman guy set him on fire?"

"Yeah," he said, smiling. She didn't return the smile, but at least Jeff had her talking again. It was a start.

"Weird place for a funeral."

"It wasn't that easy. His relatives wanted to have him buried in Louisiana. Kaufmann wanted to honor his buddy's wishes, so he and another guy got drunk and stole the body."

"You're kidding, right?"

"Nope. The body was scheduled to fly out of LAX, so they rented an old hearse and drove to the airport. Somehow they managed to convince the people there that the funeral plans had changed. So they get the coffin loaded into the hearse, still drunk as hell, then drove all the way out here. I'm not sure where, but somewhere close by they set the coffin on fire."

"Did they go to jail?"

"No. They paid a seven hundred dollar fine for burning the coffin."

The hint of a smile touched Kate's lips. It could have been painted on by the shadows or plain old wishful thinking, but Jeff thought it was real.

"So you come here and play his songs. Sort of like visiting his grave."

"Yeah. Sometimes I just need to gain some perspective."

"Why are you running, Jeff?" Her question came out of left field, and all his worries returned.

"I can't live there any longer."

"Going back to Texas isn't going to make everything better."

"No. But at least I'll be able to live on my own terms. L.A. is bad for the soul."

"L.A. isn't the problem. I don't know if you're scared of success or just restless, but you need to figure it out. You bust your ass for all these years and then when you finally get what you want, you turn your back on it? I don't understand. And what I *really* don't understand is why you couldn't just talk to me about it.

"Everything's fine and then one day you walk in and say, 'Kate, I'm moving to Lubbock,' and you just assume I'm gonna tag along."

"I didn't assume. I hoped. Look, if you don't like Lubbock, we can go anywhere. I'd even stay in Vegas with you if that's what you want. Just not L.A."

"I don't have a problem with Lubbock. My problem is with you. I want us to be together, Jeff. But you need to sort some things out."

Unsure how to respond, Jeff played another song.

ೞ

Darkness moved with predatory speed across the wide desert sky, chewing away clouds and distant bluffs. Kate pulled her legs in tighter against the growing cold, and Jeff lost himself in the music.

He sang along with the old Gibson guitar—a spooky version of "In My Hour of Darkness." It was one of the most poignant, sorrowful songs he'd ever heard, released just months after Parsons' death, and Jeff seasoned it with his own brand of failure and loss.

Kate was right. Los Angeles wasn't the problem, but it *was* a disappointing reminder of unrealized ambitions. On every corner was a nightclub where he'd labored under smoky blue lights while his soul bled out through his fingertips. Downtown was the record company office where they'd shoved money and thick contracts in his face. And somewhere in the black heart of the city was the recording studio where the producer had taken his music and twisted it—changed the arrangements, thinned out his voice, colored the sound with hazy, wet production. The end result was his very first album—a slick piece of shit that sounded nothing like him.

Weighed against his years of hard work, it was too much for Jeff to handle.

The song ended, and Jeff started another.

○₰

"What's in the duffel bag?" asked Kate when the last chord faded into silence. She was shrouded in darkness and her disembodied voice sounded soft and distant.

"The end of my career," said Jeff, unzipping the bag and dumping the contents.

"Are those tape reels?" asked Kate.

"Yep," said Jeff, staring at the flat boxes marked *Ampex*. A plastic squirt bottle of lighter fluid and a silver Zippo lay with them. The Zippo was a relic from Jeff's smoking days, but it still worked every time.

"What are you doing with them?"

"That should be obvious, right? I'm gonna burn them."

"What for?" she asked, standing up and brushing the dust from the seat of her shorts. She was obviously tired and cold and ready to leave. So was Jeff, but he had this one last thing to do.

"You're looking at the master tapes for my album."

Kate moved closer. "If you're fishing for sympathy, save the theatrics. Even I know they don't record to regular old tape anymore."

"Sometimes they do. If they want an honest to god, *warm* analog tone."

Kate released a mean-spirited laugh. "You honestly think I

believe this crap? Like you're going to just destroy something you worked six months on. Whether you like the record or not, you're not that stupid."

"It doesn't really matter if you believe me," said Jeff. He doused the tapes with the lighter fluid then thumbed the Zippo. Hungry blue fire burst from the wick. "Besides, it's more of a symbolic act than anything else. Something I need to get out of my system. It's not like the record's not already on the shelves."

"How'd you even get these?"

"Stole 'em," he said with a tired smile.

"Are you kidding? You'll get sued."

"Maybe."

"Whatever point you're trying to make is stupid. This music is all you care about. It's your whole fucking life."

Jeff's expression hardened. "*This* isn't my life," he said, pointing to the tape reels. "This is shit! All I ever wanted was this one fucking thing! Okay? Call me an idiot or whatever you want, but I put my soul into this. Every day of my life building up to *this*. Do you have any idea what it's like to work at something so hard and then have it all go to hell?"

"Yeah, I have a pretty *good* idea," she said, and Jeff flinched at the accusation in her voice.

"You of all people should understand," he said, hunched over his guitar. "You're the one always telling me not to sell myself short. Not to sell out. That's one of the reasons I come out here from time to time. To remember what's important. Gram didn't take any shit, you know? He believed in himself and the things he had to say, and he stuck to it. He wouldn't have released an album like this."

Kate sat down next to him. She leaned her shoulder against Jeff's and a pleasant chill raced up his spine.

"Dreams aren't perfect, Jeff."

"This ain't my dream. Can't you understand that?"

Kate took the lighter from him and struck it. The flame painted their faces a ghostly blue. It seemed fitting that their life together had culminated in such a dark, lonely place.

"Kate?"

"It's going to take more than burning tapes to fix what's gone wrong."

"Yeah, I know."

"Glad to hear it," said Kate, then she tossed the Zippo onto the tape boxes.

ભ

The fire didn't burn long, but it burned with intensity. Jeff stared into the flames, playing one last song, an old spiritual called "Farther Along" that his idol had recorded in the late sixties. Kate leaned her head on his shoulder, listening.

He felt guilty, having her so close again. He knew what she was thinking. She still thought he was a fighter. Now that she'd helped him banish his demons, he'd race back to L.A. to give the whole thing another shot. They'd iron out the bumps and get on with life, like this whole, misguided weekend had never happened.

She was wrong.

That city had stolen whatever fight he'd been born with,

siphoning off drops of his soul until there wasn't enough left to matter. God knows all his friends in Texas thought going to California was worse than going to Hell, and damned if they weren't right. Gram had called L.A. "Sin City," and Jeff knew it deserved the name far more than Las Vegas.

He'd given his all, and he'd been beaten.

As the fire burned, Kate's honey-sweet voice rose up in accompaniment, turning his mournful wail into something more beautiful. The flames rose with it, dancing and swaying in the cold, California air, and from somewhere far off, Jeff heard the languid sound of a second guitar. He thought at first it might be animal cries carrying through the desert night, but then the timbre of the strings rang clear, and a haunting steel guitar joined in, playing along with his lead.

Kate snuggled closer, and Jeff realized it wasn't her voice he'd heard singing. The voice came from the darkness beyond the firelight, or maybe from the fire itself. As his mind raced to catch up with this strange turn of events, a chorus of voices arose in the night like a gospel choir. The song became a dynamic, living thing—Jeff's emotions pouring from his guitar, embraced by the melancholy music of ghosts. Not knowing what else to do, Jeff kept playing.

The tiny fire that devoured his past shot skyward, now a raging red wall that shifted and swayed. Something moved at the heart of the flame, like shadows spiraling together until they took the form of a weary-eyed young man with tumbling brown hair. No mistaking him—it was Gram Parsons.

He wore a white gabardine suit embroidered with roses and

crosses, stitched with guitars. Smiling, Gram joined the chorus, and his voice eclipsed them all with its heartfelt intensity. Jeff met his gaze, never letting his guitar falter. He was afraid that if he stopped playing, it would all go away.

Jeff felt tears on his cheeks, and the sight of Gram burning with ethereal light reminded him why he'd become a musician in the first place. It wasn't a matter of choice; he'd been born with it in his soul. Just like Gram. What would he have done in Jeff's situation? Spent his life playing Lubbock honky-tonks for the pure love of the music? That didn't sound too bad. Or would he have given Los Angeles one more shot and risked more disappointment?

Hide or fight?

L.A. and Kate, or Lubbock and—what?

Jeff wanted answers, but Gram hadn't come to solve his problems. He was here to sing, to share his gift. Just a reminder that sometimes things are simpler than they seem.

When the song finally died out, the magic died with it. One second, Gram Parsons stood before him, draped in flames, the next, just the charred remains of Jeff's studio tapes smoldering at his feet.

"That was pretty," said Kate, and Jeff could tell by her tone that she hadn't shared his vision.

"Thanks," he said, placing his guitar reverently in its case. "You want to leave now?"

"Depends on where we're going," she said.

Jeff took her hand and together they walked to the car. His guitar once again stowed in the back seat, he keyed the engine to life. Kate sat quietly as it idled, waiting for an answer to her question.

Jeff put the Chevy in gear and it crept back onto the highway, headlights shining all the way to Sin City.

☙

Liner notes:

The parts about Gram Parsons in this story are absolutely true, or at least as true as events that have grown from bare bone facts into rock and roll myth can ever be.

Gram had his own thing going before joining The Byrds for a frustratingly short period of time, then went on to form The Flying Burrito Brothers. The music from this period is fantastic, but Gram's true genius comes to the fore in his pair of solo albums, *GP* and *Grievous Angel*, the latter being released months after his death at the age of 26. My favorite rock and roll song would have the be The Beatles' "A Day in the Life," but Gram's "Return of the Grievous Angel" runs a close second with it's country infused take on America's wide open spaces.

Gram's influence runs wild through the alt-country movement that erupted in the nineties and you can trace it down to any number of performers, including Uncle Tupelo (later Wilco and Son Volt), Dwight Yoakam and Ryan Adams.

If you listen to "Return of the Grievous Angel" you'll find that a post-apocalyptic Lester Bangs makes allusions to that song's lyrics in another story in this collection.

Recommended Listening:

The Byrds—*Sweetheart of the Rodeo*

The Flying Burrito Brothers—*The Gilded Palace of Sin*

Gram Parsons—*GP*

Gram Parsons—*Grievous Angel*

☙

The Review Lester Bangs Would Have Written for the New Stones Album if He'd Lived Long Enough to Witness the Fall of Humanity and the Rise of the Other

Never fear, little children. They can't keep me down for long. It's your wise old drunken uncle, reporting in live from the American jungle, tap, tap, tapping on this old Underwood with bleeding fingers and bleeding ears, hopped up on rock and roll, the very weapon that slew the old world, the very weapon that all good delinquents must some day seize by the vinyl hilt and drive right through the cold-blooded heart of the Other.

I know what you're asking. How then, in this forsaken age, does a man get a hit of that righteous shit? That bellowing, sweaty, source of all that's good and right and true. That lovely noise. Can you help me out? Cause I really just gotta have a fix so I can forget about this world of apelings and dinobeasts and goddamned lizard men with their endless fuzztone screams.

Well sit tight. Shit this good has to be shared. Roll out of your army issue cots, you drippy nosed whipsnaps, rise up and hunt down a shortwave radio like the one your old uncle has here in the bunker, the kind with needles and dials that squeals like a greased piglet and carries the murmuring verbal communiqués of the few industrious souls who haven't entirely given up on our forsaken fleshy bags of bits called humanity. They chitter and chatter about

133

the resistance, but we know the only true resistance is rock and fucking roll. We know to spin that squealing dial all the way to the left, out where the truckers, the kickers and the cowboy angels are still making music. Spin that sucker and listen in for this new world's newest band, a righteous, pissed off quartet of long hairs calling themselves The Stones.

You've heard of them?

Bullshit. Your mommies and your daddies used to sing about Honkey Tonk Women and Wild Horses, and I know that shit's stuck in your craw somewhere between the Happy Birthday song and the clack-clacking sound the apelings make when they're knocking skulls. But that band of dinosaurs is just as extinct as all the other bloated, drippy eyed beasts that were so fond of lumbering from arena to arena, sending the terminally unhip into apoplectic glee with laser show love songs and ornamental hedgerows of Marshall stacks. I firmly believe that if there's any grace to be found in this new world's ugly, untenable situation, it's that octogenarian rock stars will never again regale stadiums full of stoned oldsters with fifty year old selections from Top of the Pops.

These aren't the Stones but *The Stones*, a whip tight gathering of angry lads with an ear for blistering guitar riffs that reach out and yank the tongues right out of your drooling mouths, and the balls to assume the name of the high holy overthrown Kings of the Jungle.

You want salvation? You got it. Tune in, wait for it, and you'll hear ten pristine tracks, back to back, live, baby, live! Every night. Ten tracks, that when pulled together into a wiggling, squawking whole, form the first post-calamity punk album to bless these eternally ringing ears. And before you start yapping about how your old uncle is stuck in pre-history when kids danced and lost their virginity to needles on vinyl, let me just chime in and assure you that I don't give a fuck. I call it an album, whether that's what it is or not. I'm still one of T-Rex's Twentieth Century Boys at heart, ironic when you consider what we've got ruling over us now, but it matters not a single stoned whit what you call it. I call it an album, you call it an MP3 playlist, and your kiddies call it a serial aural implant. Makes no difference because they're all relics of a lost past. But The Stones, they're here and now, scorching your socks off and stepping up to snatch the mantle of pissed off guitar whipping gutter punks from the rock and roll void and shove it back in the scaled faces of the oppression. You want a Revolution? Stop your ineffectual whispering. It's right fucking here. The Revolution won't come quietly, it'll come as a grinding, brain chewing wall of generator-powered, distortion drenched, amplified noise! Halleluiah!

Let's dig up Joey Ramone from the bone garden and tell him his unborn grandchildren are making a racket, keeping the cave world awake with righteous rhythms, planting the fuck you flag in the belly of the conquering beast. These fab freaks don't believe in Beatles. They hate the fucking stench of teen spirit. They are their own make of madness. The Stones owe no allegiance to history's fallen cocks of the walk. Yet they have the soundtrack of your imagination firmly by the balls, squeezing all those tunes that live somewhere between memory and terror into two and a half minute audio attacks that blister your brain.

The Stones are serving notice, friends. Rock and roll may have been one of this world's bloody assassins, but it's rock and roll that's going to save us all. I know your knees start knocking every time you think about the rift. Your preachers, your newscasters and your goddamned elementary school teachers convinced you the music was nothing less than a roadmap to Satan's cage, a funeral dirge for the soul in 4/4 time. Toss granddaddy's rock into society's stewpot with all those other morsels of sin—fucking, killing, running the government—and what do you get?

The rift.

The Stones aren't like you and me. Holed up in some earthen hovel. Chasing down roaches for breakfast and if the good lord blesses us, maybe a raw mouse for dinner. They don't hang around, scratching off days on the wall and trying to remember what the sun looked like before the acid clouds wiped it from the sky. The Stones don't give a shit. They're too busy writing songs that'll give you a reason to live.

Don't think I've gone all sentimental on you. I have just as little faith in the world as anyone. But the way I see it, we only have two choices. We tenacious few can sit around wondering if that sulfurous black rift is going to keep growing until it swallows us whole, all the while hacking up monsters like some tubercular god who's begging the universe for death. Or we can catch the ass end of salvation and hang on to it for all we're worth. Tune in together for these modern prophets. Heed their wisdom. Come together on the airwaves, like we used to in our innocence. Before we knew what rock had in store for us. Before the pagan rhythms of another reality seeped into our world and poisoned the well.

The Stones understand this poison is its own anecdote.

So join me, children. Let's drink deep from the flask of heaven.

ᛞ

Liner notes:

This one has the honor of having the longest title I've ever used or will ever likely use. This is, of course, about the late great rock critic Lester Bangs who never met a rock band not named The Troggs that he wouldn't gleefully rip to shreds.

Bruce Sterling wrote the definitive story about what would have happened if Bangs hadn't overdosed while treating a cold in 1982, and if you haven't read it, "Dori Bangs" is available in one of his collections and well worth you time. I can only hope that my take on it proves to be the definitive story about what would have happened if Bangs hadn't overdosed and had lived long enough to see the world beset by "apelings and dinobeasts and goddamned lizard men with their endless fuzztone screams."

We'll see.

Recommended Listening:
MC5—*Kick Out the Jams*
Count Five—*Psychotic Reaction*
Iggy & The Stooges—*Raw Power*

ᛞ

Indie Gods

People who play it safe have no business playing rock'n'roll.
—Paul Westerberg

☙

2006

Robbie Hellerman hid from the world, trying his hardest to fill his cramped basement studio with cigarette smoke and music. The songs came, though not as easily as they had in the past, and each one left him like a chipped piece of talent falling away from what little he had left. One day he'd run out of songs, and then the need to write them would be gone. For Robbie, that day couldn't come soon enough.

He liked to imagine what Rolling Stone or Spin would have to say about his new songs if they ever got their hands on a tape. Robbie knew rock, and he understood his gift. The songs he'd written in the basement over the past several years were beautiful creations, rock and roll brilliance that outshined all the flawed but earnest musical gems that had earned him such critical acclaim in his prime. But Robbie didn't plan for the world to hear them.

The record company guy was there to change his mind.

"Did you tell me your name?" asked Robbie.

"Dusty." The guy wore an affected layer of hip that seemed informed by several generations of pop culture. Lennon's spectacles, Bolan's corkscrew hair and, God help him, a wispy goatee that looked stolen off the cover of someone's homemade grunge record. He looked to Robbie like a decidedly uncool kid, stranded in his twenties, who desperately wished he'd been old enough to see the Stones in concert before they started to suck.

"Look, Dusty. How did you even find me?"

Dusty shrugged. "I know people, right? It's not the world's biggest secret where you live."

"Guess not. But, seriously, you're wasting you time. I'm done with the music business."

"Then why are you still recording? Why'd you let me hear those songs?"

Why indeed? This kid showed up at Robbie's door yakking about the cool indie record label he owned and how he just *had* to record the first Robbie Hellerman solo record. How many of his type had Robbie kicked to the curb over the years? And yet he let the guy inside and played him a few tunes. Just a taste, but obviously enough to whet the kid's appetite even more. Robbie didn't understand why he'd done it, but he figured it had something to do with how badly he wanted someone to hear what he'd created. It was better to think of it as jonesing for an ego-struck than what else it might be—the songs themselves wanting to be heard. Wanting to lure him back into the fight.

Fuck that.

Robbie's demon hunting days were behind him.

Dusty didn't wait for an answer. "I'm not saying we'll sell a ton of copies, but you were never about that anyway, right? It's the music. People would shit if they heard these new songs. They're amazing."

"Thanks, but—"

"You know how big you are, right? You're a fucking underground legend. I mean, there wouldn't have been any Nirvana without you. No grunge, no emo, no post-punk revival. You paved the way for like a million bands."

Robbie's brain filled in what the kid left unsaid. *You guarded the rifts between earth and Chaos. You killed more dissonance demons than Mozart.*

The younger crowd was always quick to crown him as the creator of their favorite musical genre, the progenitor of the awesome and the awful. But they never gave credence to his real importance. Now matter how many rock journalists Robbie told about the Chaos of Noise and the demons, they always passed it off as eccentricity. He wasn't a rock star, not quite, but he'd been influential enough that his quirks could be tolerated.

"I appreciate the fact that you think I saved music or whatever, but I'm not recording an album for you. It's nothing against your label. I'm not recording for anyone but me."

"Mr. Hellerman, you don't understand."

"Kid, I understand everything real well. You, though? You don't understand shit."

ೞ

The opening act was a ragged looking group of kids calling themselves Unsatisfaction. We should all pitch in and buy them a guitar tuner.

Austin Live!, February 1984

ભ

1984

Robbie Hellerman staggered offstage after one of Unsatisfaction's infamous sonic disasters, banged open the door to the alley and looked for a soft place to pass out.

"Slow down." Melissa said, grabbing the collar of his tattered jacket. "You're gonna break a leg."

As if on cue, Robbie's tennis shoe hit a patch of wet cement and he slammed into the side of a dumpster. He tumbled over onto his ass and started laughing, and when the rest of the band emptied out from the club, they joined in.

Robbie grinned at them from his puddle. They swirled around, undefined shapes formed of flesh and denim, whooping and cursing the night. Melissa slid down next to him, undeterred by the rank, moldy stink that Robbie hoped was coming from the dumpster and not from him.

"They'll never let us play there again," she said, though Robbie was beyond caring. "Why are you so determined to fail?"

"What else is there to do?" he asked, still laughing. "Like I care what they think anyway." He kicked out in the general direction of the stage door, slinging water from his tennis shoe.

"Damn straight!" yelled Clyde, tossing a beer bottle into the air and leaping sideways when it shattered against the ground.

Robbie felt Melissa deflate next to him. This was an old argument, and not one Robbie felt like rehashing now. He knew damn well he was inclined to drink too much, but the other band members were no less wasted. They were lovable fuckups; that was their shtick. So what if they blew a few gigs? When they were on, they were the best underground rock band in the world. When they weren't...well, they were still rock and roll.

Besides, it wasn't like Melissa was a saint. But her "little slips" as she liked to call them where far fewer than Robbie's, and he knew better than to throw them back in her face.

"There's only so many bars we can get kicked out of," Melissa said.

Robbie scooted away from her in passive protest. "This is who we are, right? This is the band. They don't like it then we can't do much about it."

Son reached out a hand and pulled Robbie to his feet. "She ain't totally wrong. We've had better shows."

Robbie grunted, not willing to concede the point. He was vaguely aware that Melissa was right. All they ever talked about was making a record, going on tour, earning some cash. But that was never going to happen. Robbie was a drunk, Clyde was a drug addict, and Son was too much of a follower to pull either of them out of it. Melissa had a shot at saving the band, but he could sense she was growing tired of trying.

"Why are we doing this?" Melissa asked, and Robbie couldn't tell if she was talking about the band or their lukewarm relationship.

"Even drunk, we're better than *those* bastards." Clyde grimaced. The next band on the bill must have started because a muffled, tuneless howl filled the alley, like a chainsaw trying to cut through a cinder block. A high-pitched whirring joined in, and with it a sound like someone hammering glass windowpanes. It was horrible chaotic noise and even drew a nod of agreement from Melissa.

"Didn't know they let metal bands play here," Robbie said.

"Dude, you got blood on you." Son pointed at Robbie's face.

Robbie touched his nose and felt blood pooling on his lip. He was drunker than he'd thought. It wasn't the first time his stage antics had left him bleeding, but it was the first time he couldn't remember it happening. Maybe he'd hit his face when he slammed into the dumpster.

"Um, Guys?" Melissa's voice was barely audible above the growing din. She pulled a hand away from her face and revealed the blood dripping from her nose. Robbie's head began to pound and he saw looks of confusion pass across Son and Clyde's faces when they discovered they were bleeding too. The band inside the club roared against the walls and Robbie wished somebody would cut the power. He wasn't sure how anyone inside the club could stand the volume. Even in the alley, it was growing painful.

"What's happening?" Clyde wiped blood from his face with the front of his Violent Femmes tee shirt.

The dumpster began to vibrate, and the ground grew unsteady beneath their feet. The air behind Clyde rippled like a pool of water, and Robbie realized that's where the music was coming from. Clyde turned and backed away. Sound waves pulsed from the shimmering air with enough force to cause his shirt to flap. Melissa stepped in front of Robbie, like she was tying to protect him. He put an arm around her shoulder and pulled them both back in the direction of the stage door.

He didn't know what was happening, but he had a notion they didn't want to wait around to find out. "Guys. We need to leave. Now." Melissa nodded and Son said something he couldn't hear. Blood continued to pour from his nose, and the song which really wasn't a song at all, had become more abrasive and painful than ever. It sounded to Robbie like someone was drilling into his skull. It was beginning to feel like it too.

A vaguely humanoid shape emerged from the rippling air. It looked formed of shadows and static, scribbled lines of current. Every step was a hiss and a pop, every motion a brittle, dissonant screech. It had no face, no eyes to mark its intent, but Robbie didn't need an instruction manual to see it was headed toward them.

"Aw, shit," he mumbled, grabbing for the door. The others were screaming in silent voices, scattering in different directions. Melissa pointed at something, but Robbie couldn't tear his eyes away from the impossible thing that was splashing toward him through the wet alley.

Behind the creature, moonlight flickered off metal.

Then the noise howled to a stop, and the creature broke apart. Bits of whatever it was made of whipped into the air and vanished in the darkness.

A dirty man with tangled hair and a fringed leather jacket stood in the alley. He wore a wild grin and had the kind of intense eyes that made Robbie wonder if he was on drugs. One hand scratched at a graying beard, the other held a sword.

"Nice job distracting it for me," the stranger said. "All that waving your hands and running for your lives business really did the trick."

"Wait, you saw that?" Clyde said, wiping the last of the blood from his face. Now that the noise had faded, the rest of them had stopped bleeding too. "I mean, it was there?"

"It was there," Son said solemnly. "We all saw it."

"What happened to it?" Melissa asked the stranger. "What did you do?"

"Cut it in half with my blade. Sent it back where it belongs. Saved your lives. Pick whichever one you like." The stranger slid his sword into a scabbard that dangled from his hip.

"You want to tell us what that thing was?" asked Robbie.

"A dissonance demon. And not the last one you'll see."

"What's that supposed to mean?"

"It means you're marked, kid. They know you have the potential to stop them and they aren't going to wait around until you blossom. Lucky for you, I can help."

"Help how?"

"You want answers? I want food."

ങ

After a few grumbles and several strong reminders from Melissa that the stranger had saved their lives, they pooled their pocket change and ordered him a burger at the all-night diner.

When the waitress left with their order, Robbie stubbed his

cigarette in the astray and pressed the matter. "We brought you here to talk, right? So, what's the story?"

The stranger gave a disinterested shrug. "Same story as always. Chaos, Order, the delicate balance that keeps this whole plane of existence from unraveling into random bits of matter. Nasty business stopping that, but somebody has to do it, right?"

"Um, let's start with your name," said Melissa.

"Father Mastodon, at your service"

"Really?" asked Clyde, twisting up his face like he was trying to figure trig problems in his head.

"No, it's just Jim," he said, grinning. "You got your mind made up I'm a weirdo, so I figured I'd give you what you wanted."

Robbie was convinced the guy was a weirdo, regardless of his name, but he'd sobered up enough to keep from saying so. "Okay, *Jim*. What was that thing?"

"Told you, a disson—"

"Got it. A dissonance demon. What the hell's that?"

"One of the more common demons from the Chaos of Noise Tougher than a simple scream demon of course, but not the worst of them. In the hierarchy of demons they're analogous to the lesser bile demon in the Chaos of Taste."

Clyde looked to be working math again. "Am I still that fucked up, or did he just blast off some gibberish?"

"What's the Chaos of Noise? Or the Chaos of Taste?" asked Son, interest sparking in his eyes. The stranger's rambling sounded like a bunch of sci-fi shit to Robbie, but he knew that was right up Son's alley.

"I don't remember the last time I had a good cigarette," Jim said, reaching across the table with his dirty palm face up. "Nicotine helps me focus on these matters, you know?"

"We're already buying you a burger," Robbie said, guarding his pack of Marlboros. Clyde studied something on the ceiling lest he be asked to surrender one of his.

"Jeez, the guy saved our lives," said Melissa, sliding him her pack. She handed him a plastic lighter.

Jim lit up. "You are a radiant angel, my dear."

"So what about this chaos stuff?" asked Robbie.

"There are five planes of Chaos, one plane of Order. Guess which one you live in."

"I live in the plane of *you've got your bribe now get to the point*," said Robbie. "We aren't here to answer questions, you are."

Anger flickered in Jim's piercing eyes, and the sudden eruption of emotion made Robbie flinch. "I'm answering your questions, and you'd better pay attention. I'm not feeling particularly inclined to save you next time. You may have to do it yourself."

"Go on," said Son. "We're listening."

"Alright. So, humans thrive in this plane because everything's in balance. All the senses we use to process the world fit into their proper, orderly places. In the Chaos of Noise, nothing exists but sounds and they all exist at once. In the Chaos of Sight, all colors are one, darkness and light have no differences, near is far. You getting the gist?"

Son nodded. "So that...demon. It came from the Chaos of Noise?"

Jim nodded. "Yep. Chaos can't stand Order, and they're bound and determined to bring it down. It's always been that way. This world would be wiped away if it wasn't for people fighting against these other planes. People like me and you."

Robbie had an uncomfortable sense that Jim spoke this last part specifically to him.

"Imagine," said Jim, "if all the Chaos planes broke through. People would hear their food, taste their music. Widespread synesthesia. Not to mention all the demons running around chopping people in half with odors and images. Not a very happy place to live."

The waitress sat a plate with a hamburger and fries in front of Jim, refilled his water glass and left. Jim dug into his dinner while the rest of them considered his madness. Robbie wanted more than anything to believe the guy was just a nut, scamming a free meal. But he'd seen the demon in the alley. There was still blood on his jacket collar. No denying that thing was for real.

"Why us?" asked Robbie. "Case you hadn't noticed, we're not exactly equipped for fighting monsters."

"We're fuckups," said Clyde. "And proud of it."

"Music is structured noise," said Jim through a mouth full of hamburger. "Only weapon out there that will fight aural chaos."

"Forget the fact that you're not making sense," said Robbie. "Again, why us? Lots of musicians out there that put us to shame."

"Yes, but not so many with that intangible *something* that musical movements are built from. Maybe you aren't there yet, but you guys must have it in you. Otherwise the demon wouldn't have come after you."

Clyde snagged a fry from Jim's plate. "So we haven't done shit to anyone and now these things are gunning for us? That just sucks."

"Gunning for *one* of you, at least," Jim nodded. "Sometimes it's a whole band that has the potential, sometimes just one member. Either way, you better watch your back."

"Watch our backs?" Melissa seemed put out with Jim for the first time. The thick eye makeup she wore on stage had smeared down her cheek, and gravity was taking its toll on her Aquanet spikes. She was only twenty-four, but she already looked worn out by life. "The bastard could come right at my *face* and I wouldn't know what to do to stop him. Not all of us are packing swords."

"It doesn't take a sword to kill them," said Jim.

"Then what does it take?" asked Robbie.

Jim shrugged. "Depends on who you are. But in your case, it's adoration."

"Well that makes total sense," said Clyde, snatching a handful of fries as if to demonstrate his contempt. "Just tell us which end of the *adoration* you poke the thing with."

Jim gobbled another bite of his burger, sipped his water. He leveled a menacing stare at Clyde and when he spoke again, all levity was gone from his voice. "Any power you have to fight these demons comes from your fans. And especially from other musicians who emulate you. You move into bigger clubs, put out some records, and all of a sudden you'll start feeling it. It's like a drug. The rush their love sends your way. Especially on stage. Your soul stores it up like a battery, and when one of the demons pops out at you, all you have to do is let fly.

"Turn that adoration into power and take the demons down. Doesn't matter if you're holding a sword or a flower, you'll banish it back to Chaos. It's just that simple."

"Real fucking simple," mumbled Clyde.

"You embrace this destiny or you die," Jim snapped. "That simple enough for you?"

For once, Clyde was quiet. He slumped back in the booth and turned his gaze to the parking lot.

"Our destiny?" Son's bearded chin was cupped in his hands, his elbows on the table. He looked more like a kid watching cartoons that a guy learning he'd been issued what amounted to a death sentence. "What if I don't believe in fate?"

"In this case, fate is nothing more than potential," said Jim. "Fight back or don't. The demons know who you are either way. I figure you'll all be dead in a year anyway. It's just my job to make you aware of it in case you'd like to at least try to save your own asses. And maybe save the world while you're trying."

"We aren't superheroes," said Robbie.

"Nobody said you were."

Robbie's brain fired questions faster than he could hope to ask them. Who was this dude, and why was this his *job*? What did these dissonance demons see in a bunch of social rejects like them to deem them a threat? And just how soon would it be before the monsters came after them again? Finally, he seized on the question with the most immediate impact and asked it.

"Assuming we gain this adoration. How *exactly* do we use it to kill those things?"

Jim grinned like a teacher whose student had finally managed to grasp a complex equation. "A fighter, eh? There may be hope for you yet. All you have to do is hold something you can swing. I have a sword because I'm a little old fashioned about these things. You could use a tennis racket, a tree branch, pretty much anything you're comfortable with. As long as your battery is charged, so to speak, your adrenaline will cause the power of Order to slice right though your enemy. You won't have to think about it. It'll just be instinct." Jim pushed his plate away, dabbed his mouth with a napkin and slid out of the booth. "Okay, then. Now that you have the tools to give yourself a fighting chance, I have to be going."

"Hang on!" said Melissa, snatching at his wrist. "You're leaving us? What if another of those things come for us?"

"They assuredly will," said Jim, a look of wistful regret in his eyes. "Just do as I've said and hopefully you'll survive."

"Hopefully isn't very reassuring," said Son.

"Your band already has a small following," said Jim, pulling free from Melissa's grip and straightening his jacket cuff. "Shows like you played tonight will give you a small bit of power. Use it wisely until you can build a bigger following. My suggestion? Practice often."

With that, Jim started toward the door, boots clapping the tiles. He was nearly gone, then he whirled around and trotted back to the table. "Sorry, almost forgot the important part."

"Jesus, what else," said Clyde, yanking a cigarette from his pack and shoving it in his mouth.

"Don't become rock stars."

"Huh?" Robbie had grown so irritated with the man that he desperately wanted to hit him. "You told us, build a following. Get some adoration? Doesn't that equal the same thing?"

"Not exactly. The power you get comes from people loving your *music*, not loving you. If you're in it for any reason other than the music, you'll fail. You might get rich and famous, but you'll be empty superstars. It's bands that hold to their own vision that the Noise fears."

Clyde looked indignant. "So you're saying we can't sell out? 'Cause I was sort of looking forward to not being a broke bastard some day."

"You can make all the money you want, so long as you don't compromise the music. Be musicians, not rock stars."

"Don't worry, dude," Robbie scowled. "I seriously doubt that's going to be a problem."

೪

Also in stores this week, the fist full length LP release from local favorites, Unsatisfaction. My first impression was, this eponymous debut record is nothing but noise. But it rewards multiple listens. Dissonant harmony parts that sound straight off the last X album, almost buried by a rapid-fire rhythm guitar crunch that calls to mind Black Sabbath on speed. There are some gems buried in this marginally incoherent rough. Derivative? Sure. But what debut album isn't? This quartet may wear their influences on their sleeves, but there's an underlying originality to their sound. And you can't help but sympathize with songwriter Robbie Hellerman's kicked in the ass by life lyrics. At least when you can understand them.

Austin Live! Magazine, March 1985

ß

1985

The club was called Shark Attack, one of the new wave of neon bars spawning all over downtown that catered to music fans with a taste for the unclassifiable. A little pop, a lot of noise, and an independent ethos that celebrated pawn shop guitars and working class swagger. Spiked hair and buckled motorcycle jackets were at home beside skinny ties and pegged jeans. Shark Attack and its ilk didn't cater to whatever was big on the radio; they existed to serve *the scene.*

And Unsatisfaction was the scene's bleeding, broken heart.

"We're Unsatisfaction," Robbie howled into the microphone. "And you're our fucking victims!"

Melissa's base line dropped like a series of bombs behind him and Clyde's grungy old Les Paul followed her lead with a growling wall of sound. Son's snare drum hammered its way into line with the rest and Robbie colored the whole thing with ringing Telecaster notes that somehow reached into the murk and yanked out a melody, kicking and screaming.

The show was on.

Kids pressed against the stage, lunging into one another's backs, wet with beer and sweat. Hands snatched at Robbie's ankles, but he sidestepped them. Throats howled and bodies thrashed and Robbie soaked it all in like a sponge.

Charging the battery.

No one in the band had encountered a dissonance demon since the night they'd met Jim, and their would-be tour guide through the world of fucked up shit hadn't shown himself again either. If he'd have been alone, Robbie would've passed the whole experience off as a drunken hallucination. But the others had been there too, and despite Robbie's numerous attempts to sweep the experience under the rug, it was still a daily topic of conversation. It seemed like the only thing Son could talk about.

Robbie didn't buy into Jim's madness—at least that's what he told himself—so the fact that he constantly checked the shadows to see if they were shimmering irked him to no end. And if he was building the band's rep and wallowing in the attention of a growing fan base, that didn't mean he was seriously *charging his battery.* That was bullshit. This had been their goal all along, so why veer away from it just because some lunatic wanted the same thing for them?

Melissa began to sing and Robbie chimed in with a dissonant harmony part laced with reverb. The effect was spooky, even when sung over instrumental chaos. Even Robbie didn't know what kind of music they played, but he'd never been big on trying to shove music into neat categories. It rocked and people seemed to dig it. That was enough for him.

Two minutes later the song ended and Robbie yelled into the microphone. "Wind Down!"

The crowd roared and the band launched into the next song. "Wind Down" was the lead track on the indie label album they'd released in the spring. The crowd sang along—something that still made Robbie nervous and pleasantly queasy at the same time—and Robbie could feel their acceptance like a warm wind cutting the chill of obscurity. These people loved his music, loved his band. The record enjoyed modest local success, but interest was growing. Unsatisfaction wouldn't be on MTV anytime soon, but people were starting to recognize them in local record stores.

It was poor man's success, but Robbie could get used to it.

Song followed song, and the fans stayed pumped even through the tunes they couldn't sing along with. Colored lights burned his neck and the heat rising from the crowd was nearly unbearable, but this was Robbie's calling. He loved every second of it.

The demons waited until the set was nearly over to attack.

The band was lumbering through a tricked out cover of The Clash's "Brand New Cadillac" when a drawn out scratching sound cut through the din. It sounded like a phonograph needle being pulled across the world's largest record. The sound was so intense it drew screams from the crowd, and to Robbie's right, he saw Clyde drop to his knees and grab his ears.

A sound wave punched Robbie in the chest and he stumbled backward, slamming into Son's kick drum. Cymbals rang and Son jumped up from his seat as the air ripped mid-stage and spat out a pair of demons like the one that had come for them in the alley. They were fuzzy, chaotic shapes, and when they moved through the smoky air, the wash of stage lights warped around them. A smaller demon clawed through the rift between worlds and sped past his brethren.

Melissa sloughed off her bass as the thing ran at her. Blood poured from her nose and Robbie figured the same thing was happening to him. But he was far too astonished to care. Clyde was climbing back to his feet, hands still on his ears, and Robbie realized he'd been closest to the opening rift. One of the dissonance demons lashed out at him with a scribbled hand and Clyde jumped back, wailing. His guitar came off its strap and slammed into the stage, and it cried out for its owner with an endless string of feedback.

"Clyde!" Robbie disentangled himself from the scattered drum kit, dropped his guitar and moved to help his friend. He took two steps and the second dissonance demon blocked his path. Something dark burned where Robbie assumed its eyes should be, and a jagged slash widened below them to emit even more noise. Guitar feedback merged with buzzing amps, merged with the cacophony of painful noises the demons made. Bones snapping, air raid sirens, jet engines powering up.

Robbie stood transfixed, unable to run from the demon as it stepped forward and grabbed his throat. Its touch was like a buzz saw to the brain. Robbie screamed as his eardrums ruptured.

"Hang on!"

Robbie heard the words, but they sounded like they were traveling underwater. Cymbal stands tumbled at his feet, and he saw Son claw his way over the drum kit and swing his fist at the demon. Son's arm passed right through the creature, like it was made of air. Off balance, Son threw out his arms and hit the stage.

The demon let go of Robbie's throat and air rushed back into his lungs. It rounded on Son, lifted him by his legs and tossed him into the crowd. The fans surged, caught the drummer and began bouncing him on their shoulders, back toward the stage.

Oh my god. They think this is all an act.

The demon spun back around and Robbie moved behind the toppled mountain of drums, desperate to put some distance between them. His mind raced to remember what Jim had told them about fighting these things. The other demon was on top of Clyde, one hand pressing against his face. Clyde was still. The smaller creature was snapping at Melissa's ankles while she threw kicks at him that didn't land.

So we can't touch them but they can touch us?

"We are seriously fucked."

Robbie hardly realized he'd spoken, but the demon growled something unintelligible in response and moved through the drums like they were made of mist.

"Aw, fuck." Robbie scampered away from the drums, moving in the general direction of his band mates. He though maybe he could help Clyde or Melissa, though since he didn't know how to stop the thing coming after him, he wasn't sure how much help he'd be to his friends.

Then a high pitched screech bit through the din. The sound froze Robbie in place. Near the front of the stage, Melissa was stabbing the tiny demon with a microphone. Crackling blue light danced on the microphone's surface as she drove it over and over into the monster's back. The creature clawed its way across the stage, desperate to escape. But Melissa didn't relent. Another stab stopped the demon's retreat, and a final slash took off its head. A minute bit of the noise collage vanished as the demon's wavering form fell apart and bled into the shadows.

Melissa turned toward Robbie. The microphone still glowed in her hand and she held it up beside her ear, like a slasher movie killer looking for her next victim. Red stage lighting gave her a demonic glow, and for a split second, Robbie was terrified of her. Then Jim's words came back to him in a flood of memory, and he knew what he had to do.

You could use a tennis racket, a tree branch, pretty much anything you're comfortable with. As long as your battery is charged, so to speak, your adrenaline will cause the power of Order to slice right though your enemy.

Anything at all.

Robbie scampered away as the dissonance demon came up behind him. Clyde's guitar still buzzed on the floor and Robbie snatched it up. He gripped the guitar by the neck, spun around and swung it in a mad arc at the approaching demon. All sound immediately stopped. Robbie's headache retreated as a tingling sensation gripped his body. The guitar came alive with blue light and when it struck the demon, Robbie felt the contact. The monster gave a silent wail as the top of its body fell away from the bottom. Like its smaller cousin, the demon disintegrated into the darkness.

Robbie whirled around, holding the guitar like a baseball bat, and saw that the last demon was still straddling Clyde, driving its fist repeatedly into his face. Robbie moved to help him but Melissa was too quick. She brought her microphone across the back of the demon's neck. The head fell away and was gone before it hit the floor.

The blue light left Robbie's guitar as quickly as it had come, and the same thing happened to Melissa's mic. Sound returned to the world, but not the unchecked fury of the Chaos of Noise. The soundtrack for the aftermath was composed of squealing feedback, blood thundering in his head, and a sudden explosion of screams from the crowd.

"Are you okay?" Melissa fell to her knees beside Clyde and Robbie did the same. Clyde's nose was bent at a savage angle, and his face was a riot of bloody slashes. One eye was swollen shut.

"I'll live," Clyde said, sitting up and wiping blood away from his face with his shirt tail. "Probably."

The giddy crowd deposited Son back on the stage and he limped toward them, holding one arm across his chest. "What did you guys do? How'd you do that?"

"Just like Jim told us to." Melissa locked eyes with Robbie and he could read her expression. *You believe this now? You ready to take this thing seriously?*

Robbie nodded his head, though he wasn't sure what he was agreeing with.

"They think it's a fucking stage show?" Clyde said, laboring to stand.

"Then that's what they need to believe," Melissa said, supporting him with one arm.

Robbie crossed to the center microphone stand, which was miraculously still standing, and growled into the mic. "In case you forgot, we're Unsatisfaction. Now go the fuck home." He kicked the mic stand into the crowd and left the stage with his injured band mates.

The eruption of cheers in his wake was the purest expression of acceptance he'd ever experienced, and sudden warmth spread though his gut and filled his chest.

"Charging the battery," he said, throwing an arm around Son's shoulder.

The drummer winced, then grinned back at him. "So what do we do now?"

They clustered together backstage, broken but triumphant. The crowd shouted for an encore that wasn't going to happen.

"Now, we take you guys to the hospital," said Robbie. "Then we get drunk."

"Amen, brother," said Clyde. "Maybe they'll give me some good drugs."

Melissa drew her arm away from Clyde and gave him a shove. "You guys don't ever take anything seriously. Those things tried to kill us, and they'll come again. And all you're thinking about is getting fucked up?"

"That's not *all* I'm thinking about," said Robbie, gripping Melissa in a bear hug and kissing her neck. Even a near death experience couldn't completely banish Robbie's inner smart ass. Melissa wriggled free, gunned him down with an angry glare, then headed out the back door.

"What's her deal?" asked Clyde, patting his pockets in search of cigarettes. "I was just kidding. Sort of."

"She's right, though," said Son. "Tomorrow, I think we'd better practice."

"Practice our songs, or practice killing things?" asked Robbie. He watched the back door swing shut behind Melissa, feeling guilty and pissed off at the same time.

Son shrugged. "Pretty much amounts to the same thing, doesn't it?"

Cʒ

Outside, they found Melissa hunched beneath a warped aluminum awning, taking shelter from the rain. She wasn't alone.

Jim stood just beyond the reach of the awning, but the rain didn't seem to faze him. He wore the same fringed jacket that would look equally at home on the shoulders of Davy Crockett or some sixties burnout. The rain drove his stringy hair down the sides of his face and he shook his head like a dog to free it.

"I wish you'd stay gone," Clyde said, grimacing. "Every time you come around shit starts attacking us."

"I didn't summon them," said Jim, looking confused. "I was just congratulating Melissa here on slaying her first scream demon."

"Those are the little ones," said Melissa, like a student reciting something she'd just learned.

"Little, but nasty," agreed Jim, still soaking in the rain. "Told you they'd be back."

"Took them long enough," said Son. "I was beginning to think we were crazy."

Jim shrugged. "They probably though they'd take you off guard. Looks like they were wrong."

"Not hardly," said Robbie.

"Regardless. You prevailed."

"Yeah, we're real winners," said Clyde, a wadded up, bloody towel pressed against his face. "Now can I go to the fucking hospital?"

"Absolutely," said Jim. "Will you be back on your feet tomorrow?"

"I don't know. Why?"

"I'd like to begin training you."

"Huh?" Clyde staggered and Robbie caught him.

"Maybe the night after tomorrow would be better," said Jim.

"What do you mean training?" asked Melissa.

Jim's eyes lit with excitement. "When we met before, your talents were nothing but potential. Like I said, I just wanted to warn you to be ready. Now, though...now you've tapped into the power of Order. You're the real deal. Demon fighters."

Robbie laughed. This guy was too much. "Demon fighters. Right. Look, all I want is to stay the hell away from those things. Can you train us how to do that?"

"Unfortunately, no," said Jim. "Now that you've tapped into the Order, they'll be gunning for you. You'll be hunted. And not just by the odd dissonance demon or two. They'll come in droves."

Robbie's stomach knotted. "Yeah? Then we're good as dead. No kind of training's going to prepare us for that."

"Maybe, maybe not," said Jim, scooting out of the way so Robbie could lead Clyde into the rain and toward the car. "But I can help you turn the game around on them."

Robbie eased Clyde into the backseat of his rusted Pontiac. When he slammed the door, he turned back and saw Jim staring at him, pale face drawn and wrinkled, painted red by neon light. The man had never seemed so insane.

"What do you mean, turn the game around?" asked Melissa, as she and Son walked reluctantly to the car. Both of them seemed enthralled with the freak, and that bothered Robbie.

"Why wait around for them to hunt *you*?" Jim said, grinning like a skeleton. "I'll teach *you* how to hunt *them*."

ભ

Please Say You're Kidding, the second LP release from Unsatisfaction picks up where their cult-favorite debut album left off. And the band hasn't mellowed. The guitar parts are still scary enough to send your grandmother screaming into a mental institution, and the thunderstorm-heavy drums may result in a rush on new speakers to replace those they've blown apart. But this album has something its predecessor didn't. It's difficult to nail down exactly what that is, but the songwriting on this effort draws deep from the well of pop music tradition without compromising the noise palate, art punk ethos the band has spent the last few years cultivating. These songs are catchy, with melodies that jump of the vinyl and strangle the din into submission. The lyrics are still ultra-depressing, but haven't lost the wry, leavening humor that makes them bearable. This record won't get Unsatisfaction on MTV, but it might land them on some of the cooler radio stations. And it should definitely land them in your record collection. This one's worth your cash—go buy it. When the rest of the world discovers them, you can tell everyone how cool you already are.

The Daily Texan—April, 1986

ભ

1986

"So, professor. What are we killing today?"

Robbie huddled in the shadows of a recessed entryway that led into a long-vacant building. Jim crouched beside him, butt against his heels and sword balanced across his knees.

"Nothing if you don't keep your voice down," Jim said, cocking his head as if he heard something in the wind that Robbie couldn't. He'd been following Jim's lead for months now, soaking in every bit of training he could in order to keep him and his friends alive, but he still thought the guy was more that half insane.

Jim cupped a hand to his ear. "Hear that?"

"What am I supposed to be listening for?"

The city was as quiet as it ever got. Nothing moved in the empty downtown streets save for a few bits of trash pushed along by the wind, and the occasional leaf falling from the autumn bound trees. Jim taught them that the best time to hunt demons was in the neighborhood of four in the morning. The world was still then. Pure. And the demons couldn't countenance that kind of peace. If you knew what to listen for, you could catch them breaking the silence. And when that happened, you had to seize your chance.

"Listen to the wind," said Jim. "You can hear it hitting the leaves, but do you hear that whine?"

Robbie closed his eyes and concentrated. He blocked out the stench of old urine in the entryway, stilled his breathing and just listened. And there it was, carrying on the wind just at the edge of hearing, a thin whine that wasn't coming from any natural source. He could taste electricity in the air, and the hairs on his arms stood on end.

"Yeah, I hear it." Robbie cast his eyes around for his friends, but they were well hidden. He wondered if they were paying enough attention to know what was coming, and just like always, fear began to well inside him. He wasn't afraid of the demons, not on more than an instinctive level at least, but he was afraid for his friends. He'd seen what they could do to a person, what they had done to several members of Jim's supposedly well-trained team, and the thought of that happening to anyone he cared for was almost enough to sober him up.

Robbie had convinced himself that being buzzed put him in the best frame of mind for demon hunting, an opinion not shared by Jim and certainly not by Melissa. She prepared for their night prowls with the utmost seriousness, decking out in loose pants and a free flowing trench coat that gave her the widest range of motion possible without having to freeze her ass off. Jim had taught them that the demons didn't need light to see, so Melissa's dressing all in black was more of a concession to her own peace of mind than any real tactical advantage. Robbie himself generally wore whatever he'd been wearing when it was time to begin the hunt, in this case a pair of tennis shoes with the soles pulling free, tight faded blue jeans and a gray Members Only jacket draped over a striped tee shirt. The January night was cold, and he wished he'd brought more than whisky to keep himself warm.

He fished a flask from his pocket, took a swallow, and ignored the sour look it earned him.

"Focus," said Jim. "It's coming."

"I'm plenty focused," said Robbie, his voice slurred with resentment. "I know the drill by now. I know that I'd rather be getting some fucking sleep than hanging out here with you, waiting to get killed. But hell no, I'm the lucky one. I get to work all day at the record store, play a gig, then come out at this godforsaken hour when I'm supposed to be sleeping. You know, when you show up late for work, you can only tell your boss you were out demon hunting so many times before it starts to stretch the bounds of credibility."

"Stop feeling sorry for yourself," said Jim with his customary disinterest. "Just think of all that other stuff as necessary evils to advance your true calling."

"I like that other stuff. And if I lose my job, it's gonna be the landlord calling, wondering where the hell the rent is. You're so dead set on us saving the world, you need to get us a job with your gang of Order whores."

Jim bristled and Robbie smiled. He knew it irked the man that he didn't respect the Tranquility. Jim had explained to them that he was part of an ancient organization that fought Chaos with an almost religious fanaticism. Robbie thought it sounded like something out of a shitty paperback spy novel—a secret society of chosen *knights*, as Jim had called them, tasked with the elimination of Chaos and the ultimate closure of all paths between our plane and others. Robbie had laughed out loud the first time he'd heard. This hadn't pleased Jim, so Robbie seized upon any opportunity to tease him about it.

"The Tranquility doesn't pay its members," said Jim. "Inclusion is reward enough. I've explained to you that we're here to foster your kind, and if you're lucky, you may be asked to join one day."

The prospect of joining the Tranquility didn't sound like a product of luck to Robbie. "Yeah, I know. But you can at least show me the secret handshake, can't you? Promise I won't tell anyone."

"Shhhh!" Jim stood and leaned back deeper into the darkness. "They're here."

Robbie took another drink of whisky and returned the flask to his pocket. He stretched out his cramping legs and climbed to his feet. Jim was right, they were here.

The air rippled in three places, then tore with a hiss. Scream demons stepped out from each portal, knee high scribbles that immediately began fouling the air with their shrieks. It seemed they'd left the big boys at home and Robbie was grateful because that meant his nose wouldn't bleed. Getting blood out of tee shirts was tough, and wearing bloody clothes all the time was testing the boundaries of eccentricity, even for a local rock star.

Robbie heard a whoop and Clyde came running from the opposite side of the street, a bent golf club raised over his head. Clyde liked to improvise and he'd probably found the club behind a dumpster somewhere. Its flaming blue glow drew the eyes of the scream demons immediately.

"Get over here you little shits," yelled Clyde. "You're in desperate need of killing."

Jim cursed and raced toward the scream demons. Robbie laughed. Clyde was every bit as unsuited for the Tranquility's methodology as Robbie, but his wild antics seemed to be working. Their cutting screams directed toward Clyde, Jim was able to race up behind and banish one of them back to Chaos before they knew he was there. Clyde deflected the wave of their screams with his golf club, then ducked and allowed another wave to fly over his head and rip into the brick wall behind him. Clyde's eyes were wide and his face was stretched into a goofy grin. The dude was having fun.

Robbie realized he hadn't moved yet, so he bent over and picked up his guitar neck. It was an old Telecaster neck, no longer attached to a guitar, but he'd gotten in the habit of carrying it everywhere with him. He liked the feel of it in his hands, and it was light and easy to fight with. Most of his fights were the result of seeking out demons like they had tonight, but they still came for him on occasion and he liked to be ready.

When his hands touched the wood, the guitar neck came alive with blue light. It always did now in the presence of demons, and the numbing silence that resulted had become routine. The sounds of the demons fell away, but he could still hear Clyde yelling challenges at the two remaining enemies, and the whistle of Jim's sword as it bit through one of them.

Melissa jogged around the corner, a tennis racket in her hand, ready to join the fray. Son raced from the opposite end of the street, but Robbie knew it would be over before either of them arrived. The last of the demons whirled around to attack Jim, allowing Clyde to slice it in half with his golf club. The night grew silent, and the glow faded from their weapons.

Robbie continued his leisurely approach. He'd been assigned flank tonight. The guy who waits behind a few steps in case more of the baddies decided to pop out of the air. As best he could tell, though, the three of them had been the extent of the evening's threat. He'd asked Jim once why Chaos didn't send a whole shitload of them at once, a whole army to kill them all.

"That's what they want to do," Jim had answered, face tightening. "But it takes a great deal of power to break through from Chaos to Order. A little rip here, a longer tear there. That's all they can achieve now. But every demon that tastes the air over here takes the memory of Order back with him, and they understand it a little more. If they ever achieve true understanding, you'll see an army all right. And that'll be that."

"Why do we hunt them then?" Robbie asked. "We're just sending them back to Chaos with another piece of the puzzle."

Jim gave a weary shrug and looked to Robbie like a man on the edge of losing hope. "The alternative is to let them run wild. What else can we do?"

"Has anyone ever thought of taking the fight to them?"

"Yes they have."

"And?"

"And they died. Badly."

Jim hadn't been willing to discuss it further, and Robbie had let it drop. He wasn't an ambitious man, and seeking out demons on this plane was more than enough work for him. Now, it seemed to be getting easier. True, they hadn't faced any dissonance demons tonight, and thankfully no rage demons, but even with Clyde's antics, the banishing had been carried off with a startling degree of efficiency. Robbie wondered if they were getting good at this.

"You're just a big bumbling child," Jim said to Clyde as Robbie and the rest reached the middle of the street. "How can you make a game out of something so dire?"

"Dire?" Clyde leaned on his crooked golf club and almost lost his balance. His eyes were wild, brimmed with red, and his body was filled with ticks. The results of too much speed maybe. But at least he'd stopped fucking around with the heroin. "What's dire about those little guys? Hell, they're kind of cute."

"Their screams can rip you in half."

"Yeah, if I let them hit me. I don't plan to."

Jim pressed his lips together, likely realizing that he couldn't win an argument with Clyde. Not if logic was his weapon.

Clyde grinned, not ready to let it go. "You like that sweet slashing move I made, saving your ass? You think them Tranquility cats will let me join the club when they hear about that? I'm a pretty tranquil motherfucker."

Jim sheathed his sword, ignoring Clyde's jabs. "They're gone, in any event. The frequency I heard was purely scream demon. Did anyone hear a dissonance demon's arrival tone?"

"No," said Son, and they all agreed. The low frequency rumble of an arriving dissonance demon was much easer to hear than the scream demons' whine, and they were much more accustomed to it.

"I'm up for more if anyone else still wants to hunt," said Melissa, tennis racket under one arm.

"I'll play," said Robbie. In truth, he wanted to go home and sleep. But he'd felt Melissa begin slipping away from him lately, and was eager to get back in her good graces. It wasn't that they'd been fighting exactly—no more than usual anyway—but a wall of apathy was growing between them, and Robbie had been wondering if they stayed together only because it was expected of them. Robbie loved her, but the relationship was still a challenge.

Robbie's parents had stayed married way too long, the way married couples often do for the sake of their children. Robbie was afraid he and Melissa had reached a similar situation, but they were still together for the sake of the band.

"So, Mr. Hellerman's not a wuss," said Melissa, grinning. Robbie couldn't help but smile back at the hope that smile gave him. "What about the rest of you?"

"I'm a willing participant to the slaughter," said Clyde. "Assuming I can stand that long."

Son didn't look ready to assume anything, and he slung an arm around Clyde's back to steady him. "I think you've bagged your limit, dude. How about I lead you somewhere you can pass out and we leave the demon killing to those of us sober enough to walk without assistance."

"Leaves me out," said Robbie and instantly regretted it. Melissa's jaw tightened.

Nice work, asshole.

He was only mildly drunk, but should have known better than to joke about it. Quickest way to piss her off was to remind her that he was unwilling to part with his vices.

"I think we've all had enough," said Jim, reaching into his jacket pocket for a smoke. "Tomorrow night, after your gig?"

"Aw, shit no," said Robbie. "I gotta sleep."

"We'll be there," said Melissa. She gave Robbie a hard stare, as if challenging him to argue.

Robbie took the bait.

"We can't do this every night. We've got to have some time to unwind."

"You mean some time to get fucked up, right? Doesn't look like hunting is getting in the way of that."

"God damn, I'm tired of this shit. Can we argue about something else for a change?"

"Not a problem! I know plenty of things we can argue about. Let's start with—"

Jim slapped a hand over Melissa's mouth. It shocked them all, and Robbie would have pulled him away from her if he hadn't seen the fear in Jim's eyes. He made a shushing sound, and cocked his ear to the sky. Their training kicked in, and the band did likewise, wondering what Jim was listening for. The night sounded normal. No booms, no whines, nothing but the constant swish of leaves blowing across concrete.

Maybe a little *too* constant.

"Run!" yelled Jim, shoving them out of the deserted street and toward the sidewalk.

None of them waited for an explanation. Even Clyde mustered the sobriety to break into a run.

The swishing sound intensified and Robbie heard the familiar ripping of reality that signified something else had crossed through. Clyde and Melissa were in front of him, Son and Jim just behind. Still running, Robbie cast a look back and instantly regretted it.

The demon had appeared in the street a few feet from where they'd been standing, and it was unlike any of the others they'd seen. It was composed of the same scribbled sound waves and white noise as the others, but it was huge. Easily twice as tall as a dissonance demon, and only vaguely humanoid, it seemed formed of random clumps that refused to keep a constant shape. Arm-like protrusions grew and withdrew, reached and retracted as it propelled itself forward, giving chase. Robbie would have screamed, but the sound might have given the creature strength.

He noticed their weapons were glowing, and wondered what the hell they were supposed to do with them. Jim hadn't told them anything like this existed, and he seemed just as freaked out as the rest of them.

Clyde led them around the side of an abandoned restaurant, into a nearly empty parking lot. Yellow street lights buzzed overhead. The footsteps died behind him and Robbie spun around to see that Jim and Son were no longer following. They held their weapons in front of them as the thing lurched toward them.

Crazy bastards are making a stand.

Ahead, Melissa was helping Clyde negotiate a path between two closely parked cars. Neither of them were looking back, and Robbie hoped that when they cleared the cars, they'd keep running.

No sense all of us dying tonight.

Robbie choked up on his guitar neck like a baseball bat and ran back toward the demon. The massive creature radiated such high-pressure sound waves, that Robbie felt like he was running through water. He was desperate to help his friends, but it was like one of those uncomfortable dreams where no matter how fast you run, you never seem to get anywhere. When he'd passed half the distance between himself and the monster, an explosion rocked the air. The demon had focused a sound wave, sending Son hurtling back through the air. His body went limp when it struck a scarred brick wall. Son fell to the ground and Robbie's heart lurched when he saw the thin streak of blood spattered against a canvas of graffiti art. Some wit had painted a reasonable facsimile of Ronald Reagan with devil horns, but now the leering President's eyes were gone. Blinded by Son's blood.

Robbie wanted to go to his motionless friend, but he knew if he didn't find a way to take out the monster, they'd all end up the same way.

Jim ducked as the thing lunged at him with one of its arms. The self-proclaimed Knight of Tranquility brought his sword over his head and neatly severed the arm. Dropping to a crouch, he whipped the sword around and made contact with the thing's body. It screeched and blew Jim back a few steps, but Robbie took heart in the fact that it couldn't cause sonic booms at will and toss them all around like rag dolls. Jim was all business now, wrenching the sword free, rolling away from another of the demon's lunges, and taking away another of its arms with a vicious slash.

Suddenly, some of the pressure the creature was exerting faded and Robbie lurched forward, nearly tripping over his own momentum. He raised his weapon, swung it at the demon and found only empty air. The creature brought its arm underneath his swing and grabbed his waist in a massive paw. The protection his powers afforded him to resist the demon's aural assault dropped like a falling scrim and Robbie screamed his way from daydream to nightmare. He was all but certain that his brain was melting from the pain and he had nothing left to wish for but an immediate death. Blood ran freely from his nose and he began praying for life to stop. Even an eternity in Hell would be preferable to what he was feeling.

Then it stopped, and Robbie was on his knees gasping for breath. The creature wailed and Robbie placed an unsteady hand on the guitar neck in front of him. He couldn't remember dropping it, but its touch returned the mercy of silence. He raised his head and saw Jim, still a dervish of slashes and back steps, lunges and parries. Robbie was astonished at the man's fighting ability, and for the first time he wondered if there was more value to the man's secret society than he'd given him credit for.

Robbie stood, fighting back the pounding in his skull. The creature was occupied again with Jim. The knight had taken off most of the demon's arms, and Robbie decided it must have been Jim who cut him free. Unnoticed, Robbie steadied his weapon and drove the head into the creature's side, tuning keys and all. He yanked it back with an upward swipe and giggled when he saw the long tear he'd opened in the demon's body.

"You like that shit?" he yelled, losing his mind in the moment. "You like it?"

Jim severed another arm then followed Robbie's lead, dipping his sword in and out of the monster's hide. Nearly armless now, it attempted to roll away, but the attackers gave it no leeway. With an animal howl, Robbie plunged his weapon into a blurry spot that he assumed was its head, and the guitar neck ended the thing's life. A silent explosion of sound particles took to the air, and then only Robbie and Jim remained in the parking lot, breathing heavily and grinning at each other, flush with victory.

Then Robbie remembered Son.

"Aw, shit."

He trotted toward his fallen friend. Melissa had already reached Son and had pulled him into a sitting position. Makeup streaked down her face, but she wore a relieved smile that stripped away much of Robbie's concern.

"What the hell was that?" asked Son, struggling to stand. He held a hand over the back of his head, and enough blood was pouring out between his fingers to cause Robbie to worry again.

"Hospital. Now." Robbie said, still trying to catch his breath, and Melissa nodded. She gave Robbie a curiously soft look, and he repaid her with a smile. Together, they lifted son and began walking him up the block to the place where they'd parked their car. Clyde arrived just as they were leaving, face pale like he was either scared shitless or had just finished throwing up. He stumbled along behind them.

Robbie had a thousand questions for Jim, but the fight had formed something new between them. An understanding of sorts. Robbie waited, knowing Jim would provide him answers in due time.

"What was that?" Son asked again. His brain was stuck on repeat and Robbie couldn't blame him.

"Don't talk," Robbie said. "First thing's first."

"First thing is, why didn't Sir Jim here tell us about things like *that*?" A bent cigarette drooped from Clyde's mouth; he hadn't even bothered to light it. Robbie understood he was scared, but he thought Clyde was a little to accusatory for a guy who'd managed to avoid the entire scrape by virtue of being a fuckup.

"Who cares," Robbie snapped, although he was wondering the same thing. "It's dead and Son's not. Let's keep it that way."

The wail of sirens grew in the distance and Robbie flinched. He'd been growing more and more afraid of simple sounds, and tonight's episode would probably do him in for life. But Jim was relaxed and he knew it wasn't demons headed their way. It was cops.

He hurried them along. Talking to cops was an iffy proposition on a good day, but today there would be too much he couldn't explain.

Robbie had asked Jim once why the demons rarely manifested when others were around. Their assault on the band at Shark Attack had been out of the norm, and in all their evenings of demon hunting, only one person had seen them fight. A homeless dude named Marco, a fixture on the local street scene thanks to his cryptic way of speaking, his quasi-Victorian dress, and the miniature Chihuahua named Elvis that always followed at his heels.

Marco had poked his head out of a dumpster one night just as Robbie had taken off a dissonance demon's head. Far from afraid, Marco had given him the thumbs up sign before returning to his dumpster diving. As far as Robbie knew, the man had kept their secret.

"They hate the silence," Jim had explained. "So they seek the quiet places to disrupt. The attack at the club was a calculated strike to take you out. Once they realized you'd come into your powers, a frontal assault was no longer worth the attempt. You know what that means?"

"What?" Robbie asked.

"Means when they come for you again, they'll be sneaky about it. So don't be caught slacking."

The sirens drew nearer as the gang helped Son off a curb and onto a narrow street between two abandoned buildings. The car was where they'd left it. A man sat on the hood, one long leg bent back so his cowboy boot rested on the grill. A wide brimmed hat shadowed most of his face, but didn't hide his insolent smile. When he saw them, he stood and began walking toward them; his blue leather coat twisted behind him when he moved, and it rang with the sound of bells and clanking metal.

"Where've ya'll been?" he asked. "Some of us have places to be."

When Jim saw the man, he threw an arm against Robbie's chest and halted his progress. Son groaned at the sudden stop and Robbie took on more of his weight.

"Get away from here," Jim said. At first, Robbie thought Jim was speaking to him, then Jim drew his sword and advanced a step toward the approaching stranger. Robbie wanted to follow, but he doubted Son would be standing long without him.

The stranger stopped just beyond sword swinging range and grinned. "Jim Weathers? Hell, ain't nothing killed you yet?"

"If you leave now, you take your head with you," said Jim.

"You never was the sociable type," said the stranger. "But I don't remember you being rude."

Jim answered with a quick stab. The sword jumped forward and the stranger danced back a step, coat ringing in the wind.

"Well damn you too," said the stranger, looking genuinely hurt. "I didn't come here to kill you or anything. I'm just supposed to bring you a message. Besides, we was friends once. No need to go around waving that sword at me."

"Give your message and leave," said Jim.

Clyde managed to slip up next to Jim and give the stranger his best go-to-hell scowl. "Who the hell are you?"

"Clyde. Step away," said Jim. There was no hint of reprimand in his voice, but it was evident he didn't think Clyde a match for the cowboy.

The stranger tipped back his hat brim and glared at Clyde like he'd just noticed Jim wasn't alone. "Who'd you piss off, Jim? Never knew the Tranqs to waste you on a sorry lot like this."

"You wouldn't be here if that's what you thought of them. Give me the message and go."

"Fine," said the stranger, throwing up his hands in mock disgust. When he did, Robbie noticed the gun belt around his waist and the pair of revolvers dangling from his hips. "The Noise wants you to stop hunting its servants."

"No shit?" sneered Clyde. "Well I'm glad you told us. Otherwise we might have wasted more time saving the world."

The stranger gave Clyde a hard look. "You're goddamned pathetic. What makes you think you can save the world?"

Jim cut off any potential retort from Clyde. "You've had your say, Clement. Now go."

"That ain't all the message," Clement said. "The Noise will forget about your little gang here. It'll stop coming for them if they stop hassling its boys."

Jim laughed. "Somebody's scared."

"Somebody's cocky." Clement backed away a few paces and the air began shimmering behind him. Robbie instinctively reached for his guitar neck, but it wasn't glowing.

"Is that what you get for selling your soul?" asked Jim, his sword still between himself and Clement. "They let you use their portals?"

Clement shrugged. "Fringe benefits."

The air ripped behind him and he backed into it.

"Hey, Jim," said Clement, his words and body both becoming blurred. "I never did like you much."

Clement's gun was in his hand so fast, Robbie never saw his coat move. Jim lunged forward but the bullet tore through his arm before he could reach the vanishing cowboy.

Son jerked free from Robbie and Melissa's grip and hit the street.

The portal closed with a sharp zipping sound and Clement was gone.

"Son!" Melissa shrieked and fell to her knees. Robbie dropped down beside his friend and saw the fresh wound in his chest. Son jerked, trying to roll onto his side and blood poured out beneath him.

"Call the fucking ambulance!" yelled Melissa, but it sounded like they were already on their way. The sirens wailed like servants of the Noise, and the street became bathed in alternating blue and red light. Robbie gripped Son's hand and watched his friend's desperate struggle for breath. Nearby, Clyde was howling along with the sirens, kicking the car and throwing his fist into the brick wall over and over.

"Son, you are not gonna die," whispered Robbie, but he knew it was a lie.

Suddenly the cops were everywhere. Clyde's face was against the wall, his hands cuffed behind his back. They pulled Melissa and Robbie to their feet. Robbie was numb, and he allowed himself to be led to a police car, head cocked back for a last look at his dying friend. Melissa continued to scream as she fought to claw her way free from the police.

A med team trotted past Robbie but Son wasn't moving. A heavy hand shoved Robbie's head into a cop cruiser, and he shut his eyes against burning tears. When he opened them again, he peered through grimy windows and saw Melissa being dragged off. Clyde was sitting against a brick wall, banging his head against it.

Jim was gone. Somewhere in the madness, he'd vanished jut like the cowboy.

cs

Shielding his eyes with a pair of scratched aviator sunglasses, Robbie stepped out into the midday sun. It was one of his rare forays into the real world since Son's death, but he was hung over and jonesing for coffee, and he couldn't milk the old coffee grounds another day. Melissa walked with him, thin and tired in her tank top and wrinkled skirt. Clyde was passed out on their floor and any attempt to wake him would have been useless.

Robbie hoped they didn't run into anyone they knew.

Unsatisfaction had become notorious overnight, but it wasn't something he relished.

Three weeks after the murder, and the emotional scab was still sore and bleeding. Every time one of his fans asked what had really happened, or every time one of his friends called to offer weak consolations, Robbie felt like he was once again in that parking lot, watching his friend flail against the pavement. And the worst part of it was, he had no idea who had killed him.

He knew the face, could pick the guy out of a lineup. In fact, he and Melissa and Clyde had all described the guy to the cops. But what good did that do them? The cops wouldn't be looking for the killer in the Chaos of Noise. They only half believed a member of the band didn't kill Son. They'd sworn to the cops that Son was fighting off a highly agitated dude who'd tried to mug them, and he was shot in the scuffle. Their story had some holes, but there was no gun at the scene and no way to prove anyone in Unsatisfaction had anything to do with it. Robbie was pretty sure the cops thought they were lying, but telling the truth might land him in a mental ward.

Robbie and the band had yet to play another gig, or even discuss the possibility of replacing Son on drums. But they'd kept close to one another. Clyde often stayed over at Melissa and Robbie's apartment, drinking himself to sleep and trying to hide the fact that he was practically living on cocaine and speed. Robbie was drunk more often than not, and Melissa had made no effort to stop him.

"We have a show scheduled at Under Over in two weeks," Melissa said. "The release party."

Robbie nodded. He didn't want to think about it. Their third record would hit the shelves within the month, and he wasn't sure he could even listen to it. Worrying about the band's commitments made his head hurt worse.

"We can't break in a new drummer that fast," said Melissa.

"We don't need a new drummer."

"We'll have to get one at some point."

"Why?" asked Robbie. He was in no mood to think about the band.

"Because we're going on tour. We can cancel club gigs, but we can't back out of the tour. We might not get another shot. It's hard as hell to think about. I know. But Son would kick our asses if he thought we were gonna blow this chance."

Robbie's face flushed and he thought about screaming something about Melissa not having a fucking clue what Son would want, but he knew that wasn't true. She'd known Son longer than he had, and they'd always been close. Close enough that Robbie's unreasonable jealousy had sparked on a few ugly occasions.

They bought matching coffees from the convenience store, and walked down to the edge of the river that cut through downtown. The grass was cool and they sat together, watching people row by in rented canoes.

After a few minutes of silence, Robbie spoke. "I'm not sure how much I care about the band anymore."

Those words might have earned him a tongue lashing from Melissa a few weeks ago. The band was her life, and she took it far more seriously than the rest of them. But she looked at him with sadly beautiful eyes.

"Neither do I, to tell the truth. But that doesn't matter."

"How come?"

"Because we've got to pull ourselves out of the shit. We've got to go on this tour."

"Not to sound like a broken record—"

"It's like this," she said. "We let the band go down the toilet and we lose our ability to fight the demons."

"Fuck the demons!" Robbie shoved up from the grass and hurled his half-empty coffee cub at the river. "Let somebody else chase after them. Let somebody else fucking die."

"Somebody else maybe doesn't have the talent you do."

"Me? Shit, you're twice the songwriter I am."

Melissa stood up and took his hands in hers. "Thanks for the pep talk. But this band has always revolved around you. You're the spark that drives it all. The rest of us are important parts of the music, and probably the magic. But you're the core. Haven't you figured that out yet?"

"That's bullshit."

"Maybe. But it's the truth."

A rustling in the grass alerted Robbie to an approaching figure. The fringed jacket was gone but Jim had replaced it with an ankle length rain coat. His face was more drawn than usual and his eyes haunted rather than insane. The sunlight didn't agree with him, and Robbie realized he'd never seen the man during the day.

"Where the fuck have you been?" Robbie dropped Melissa's hands and stalked up the embankment toward Jim. His fists clenched and he fully intended to beat the guy blind. He might be some kind of ninja swordfighter, but Robbie needed to hit him just once. One blow for Son, and for all the truths the asshole had conveniently forgotten to tell them. But when he reached the spidery live oak that shaded Jim from the sun, all of his anger bled away and he was left with a feeling of utter hopelessness. Smashing in the guy's face would accomplish nothing, and he was quickly becoming aware that the same could be said for most of his actions.

"I though you might need some time," said Jim.

"That's real thoughtful of you."

Melissa came up behind him and looped an arm though his. She'd always been the one most eager to follow Jim's lead, to learn from him. But standing on the riverbanks with their world falling apart, she studied the man like he was something she'd found clogging her sink. "We're not ready to go hunting again, so why don't you just leave. You've got that part figured out, right? I didn't see you anywhere near the police station that night."

Jim looked nonplussed. "What could I have done? I assume you didn't tell the police the truth of the matter."

"We don't *know* the truth of the matter," said Melissa, her voice growing sharp. A few curious joggers glanced their direction, then passed by. "You left before telling us anything. Some friend of yours pops out of the air, kills our friend, and you just take off."

"Clement is *not* my friend," Jim said.

"Sorry," said Melissa, scowling. "Your *ex* friend."

"Would you like answers, or would you prefer to make yourself feel better by insulting me some more?"

Robbie grabbed Jim's ratty hair and yanked the man toward him. Jim's hand fell to the hilt of his sword, but Robbie knew he wouldn't draw it. People were all around him, many already staring at them. Not to mention the fact they were important pawns in the Tranquility's war against Chaos.

"I suggest you lose the attitude," Robbie said. "You're the one's been hiding out for almost a month. You're the one who forgot to tell us some of the bad guys might be carrying guns. And I have a feeling you've forgotten to tell us a whole lot of other things we need to know. Now, you want to chat?"

Jim glared at Robbie, then nodded. Robbie relased his hair and shoved him away.

"The man who killed Son is named Jackson Clement," Jim said with no further preamble. "He used to work for the Tranquility. He rubbed some people the wrong way and was released from duty."

"So he jumped ship to the other side?" Melissa asked.

"Yes. He's a member of the Disharmony. They're an ancient cult that worships Chaos. All that we're fighting against, they're fighting *for*. I can't put it in plainer terms than that. I don't believe Clement really worships Chaos. I think he joined the Disharmony just to spite our side."

"Doesn't really matter his reasons," said Robbie. "Son's still dead."

"Yes he is," said Jim. "And I'm sorry I didn't give you a warning. But what would you have done?"

"Maybe bring a gun or something," said Melissa.

"Let's lay it all on the table," Jim said. "We're working with long odds here. The planes of Chaos keep getting stronger, and people like you who can fight them are getting scarcer. There's not much chance we can win out in the end. Add to that a group of fanatical humans hunting down the few of you with the gift, and becoming a Knight of Tranquility doesn't have much to recommend it. Sorry I didn't tell you, but my job is to train people like you, not scare them off."

"So that's it?" asked Melissa. "Nothing else up your sleeve."

"That's it," said Jim.

"Good," said Melissa. "Then we're done with you."

She grabbed Robbie's hand and he followed her up the embankment and toward the maze of skyscrapers and filthy streets that somehow coexisted with nature.

"Wait," Jim said, trotting up behind them. "What do you mean?"

"We may keep fighting Chaos," Melissa said, never slowing her pace. "That hasn't been decided yet. But whatever we decide, you're no longer a part of it. Go back to your buddies, sharpen your swords, do whatever it is you do when you're not fucking up people's lives. But if you stick your face in our lives again, I can promise I've hunted my last demon."

Robbie kept quiet, but he gave Melissa's hand a supportive squeeze. Jim stared at them with his mouth open, like he knew he should say something but was afraid Melissa would make good on her threat. Melissa and Robbie turned away and walked back to their apartment.

Jim didn't follow.

ଔ

Controversy surrounds the release of Unsatisfaction's third full length LP, Ear Pollution. *Drummer Eric "Son" Mitchell was gunned down last month and the killer has yet to be found. This tragedy is the latest escalation in this troubled band's litany of legal problems. Public drunkenness, assault, vandalism, and alleged drug usage all color the legend of one of Austin's most popular bands. For the last year, Unsatisfaction has seemed destined to leap into the national spotlight, but with an opening slot on this summer's R.E.M. tour, they may finally get their shot. Yet local supporters are familiar with the coin-flip nature of Unsatisfaction's live shows. They perch somewhere between brilliance and ineptitude, and the scale can tip either way on any given night. When sober and in the right frame of mind, they're one of the greatest rock bands to ever take the stage. Other nights, one just hopes they're able to make it through the set without falling off the stage.*

The R.E.M. tour may be make-or-break for Unsatisfaction, and fans are hoping they can harness their demons long enough to show the rest of the world what Austin has known for years. Unsatisfaction is the best band no one's ever heard of. When they want to be.

So what about the album they'll be touring behind? That's the good news; it's stunning. There's a new vulnerability to bandleader Robbie Hellerman's crystalline guitar leads, and a burgeoning maturity to his vocals. This is the album we all knew they could make, and I don't mean that as an indictment of their past albums, but instead a testament to what they've achieved here. All of Unsatisfaction's staples are here—multilayered, growling guitars, vocal harmonies that swirl together with equal parts beauty and violence, and keening, dramatic Telecaster leads that tie the whole beautiful mess together with an impossibly original bow. Unsatisfaction mines every ounce of promise from their two previous LPs and turns it into ten heartfelt, angry, lovelorn, and violent songs that are unlike anything you've ever heard. This may be the album of the year, and one can only hope that this troubled band grabs this opportunity with both shaking hands and holds on for dear life.

A replacement hasn't been found for Mitchell, but Unsatisfaction is scheduled to play an album release party at Over Under (5th & Lamar) this Saturday night. Little Lover and Speak No Weevils open, doors at 9:00. This will be your last chance to see Unsatisfaction live until after their summer tour, and based on the strength of this record, possibly your last chance to see them in such a small venue. Get there early, and cross your fingers that Hellerman and company are able to play their instruments.

You might just see the best rock band on the planet.

Austin American Statesman, June 1987

 CS

1988

Dust and smoke mingled in the growing sunlight that struggled through the hotel room's gauze curtains. Skinny and shirtless, Robbie sat on the edge of the bed, picking his way through possible melodies on his scratched up acoustic guitar. The perfect bridge for the song he'd been trying to write had proven elusive, and he'd spent much of the night searching for it. But the hunt for perfection was part of the fun, and he knew from experience he'd catch his prey eventually.

Melissa slept beside him, covers pushed down to reveal the tops of her breasts. Sweat beaded on her neck and matted hair lay across her face as she turned in fitful sleep. They were in some part of Florida—Tampa, Miami maybe; it was hard to keep track. All Robbie knew was the air was too humid to reasonably support any life but fish and bugs, and he'd chosen to spend the night writing songs instead of tossing around in bed hoping the air conditioner might magically fix itself.

Being a rock star was glamorous work.

Robbie stubbed his cigarette and lit another. He sipped a cup of cold coffee. He'd been sober for six months, and he hardly missed it any more. They were knocking out audiences every show and losing his Jack Daniels habit had actually improved his songwriting. He'd secretly feared it would be the opposite.

He picked out a few broken melodies, then settled on a cool sounding lick in D-minor. Not exactly what the song needed, but closer.

Warm arms slid around his chest and Melissa sat up behind him. "How long have you been up?"

"Never went to bed."

"Play that part again. It sounded nice."

"It's nice. But it's not perfect."

"What is?" Melissa asked. "It works in the song. You're the big Sex Pistols fan. You think they cared about perfect?"

She got out of bed, pulled on a pair of black panties and an oversized Sonic Youth tee shirt, and ran some water for a fresh pot of coffee.

Robbie played the lick again, drifted into a slow, improvised lead part. By the time he smelled the coffee, he'd decided it was maybe a little better than he'd thought. Melissa was right. It might do.

She climbed back on the bed, pulled her knees up to her chin and sipped her coffee. "You think Clyde's awake?"

Robbie snorted. "I just hope he's alive."

Last they'd seen Clyde, he'd been wandering around in the hotel lobby with a short brunette who hadn't been able to remember her own name. Both were obviously fucked up, and Robbie had somehow convinced them they should make their way to Clyde's hotel room instead of annoying the night clerk and possibly getting themselves tossed in jail for being general pains in the ass. Clyde and the woman sang a medley of Unsatisfaction tunes at top volume all the way to his room, and Robbie made sure they were safely locked away before heading to the room he and Melissa shared next door.

Clyde's continued drug abuse was one of the few dark spots on an otherwise career-making tour. Son's death had given Robbie's personality a serious makeover, but it had only driven Clyde further away from the rest of the band. Melissa made a habit of hiding his stash whenever she could sneak it away from him, but it was impossible to watch him every hour of the day. Clyde was sneaky.

"Jesus, my back hurts," said Melissa, grimacing. "I haven't been tossed against a wall in a long time. I was kind of getting used to not being in pain."

"I got revenge for you," Robbie said, grinning. "Poked him in the eye."

Melissa laughed and blew him a kiss. "My hero."

"It was the least I could do for the lady who chopped up that weird ass snaky looking dude that tried to rip my leg off."

"He was feisty."

"Most of them are."

"Yeah, but he *really* wanted to take off that leg. Bastard shouldn't have messed with it," said Melissa. "Don't they know you're *my* bitch?"

"Not sure. Maybe we should send out a memo."

Melissa smiled and sat her steaming coffee cup on the nightstand. She scooted over next to Robbie and kissed his cheek.

"Are we crazy for doing this? Does it even make a difference in the world?"

"Guess we can quit and find out."

Melissa pressed a cheek against his arm. "No. It sounds weird, but I think I actually like the hunt. I used to do it because they were coming for us and it pissed me off. And I did it because Jim guilted us into it with all that *heroes saving the universe* shit. Now I just like the fact that we're maybe making the world a better place. That and I like that cute zippy sound they make when their heads come off."

Robbie laughed and leaned his guitar against the bed. He moved to sit cross legged on the bed in front of Melissa, pale flesh peeking out through the holes in his jeans. He grinned at her, sharing the silence and their great unifying reason for being. What she was saying didn't sound weird to him at all. After giving Jim the big kiss-off, they hadn't made any conscious decision to resume their demon fighting. They'd simply decided to roam the streets one night, ostensibly to find an all-hours club and listen to some music, but instead they'd fallen back into hunter mode without even knowing it.

Their purpose was unspoken, but they shared it nonetheless. Their bond had intensified even more due to the fact that Clyde had sworn off demon hunting and just about everything else in the world other than playing guitar, shooting up, and fucking whoever was waiting for him after the show. Now they hunted alone under the streetlights, and every demon Robbie sent back to Chaos gave him a feeling of accomplishment. Like he was giving them a big fuck you from Son.

Robbie and Melissa had never been closer, and as they sat together, bathing in muted Florida sunshine, he realized he'd never told her he loved her. He wasn't sure he'd even been aware of it himself until that second, but all of a sudden it seemed like he'd felt that way for years and just hadn't known how to express it.

"It's a good thing we do," he said, taking hold of her hands.

"Entertaining a bunch of heathens with our devil music?" She winked and nudged him with her toes.

"That too."

Sirens howled in the distance, and the room was growing hotter every second the sun rose higher, but Robbie was in a state of utter peace. He pulled Melissa close to him. She smelled like coffee and hairspray and detergent from her clean tee shirt. He inhaled against her neck and she laughed.

"What are you doing?"

"Just glad we're here," he said. "I love you, Melissa. You know that, right?"

"How could you not?" she asked, but when she pulled away and looked at him, he saw her green eyes were wet. "You're pretty loveable yourself."

"So I've been told," he said.

She pinched his stomach and he leapt back. She continued the attack, pinning him back on the bed and holding his arms down with her hands.

"Careful," he said, not making much effort to free himself. "I'm delicate."

"Better shape up, then. I don't care for delicate boys." She pulled at his zipper and he slid away from her grip.

"I'm not that easy," he said, scampering away. She lunged at him, laughing, and the weight of her against his chest sent them both tumbling off the bed and onto the ground.

"See," said Robbie. "Now you've broken me."

"Nothing that can't be fixed," said Melissa. She was on top of him again and kissing him. This time, when she reached for his zipper, he didn't stop her. Seconds later, her tee shirt was tossed on top of Robbie's crumbled pants, and they enjoyed their last minutes of pure happiness before the world kicked them in the face again.

Robbie was just sliding back into his jeans when the cops knocked on the door.

CR

Clyde Owens, guitar player for the Texas rock band, Unsatisfaction, was found dead in a Ft. Lauderdale hotel room last week. Cause of death is believed to be a drug overdose. The band was in the middle of a scheduled 27 city headlining club tour, following a successful stint last summer opening for R.E.M. Controversy has often surrounded Unsatisfaction, including the still unsolved murder of their original drummer, Eric Mitchell, last year. Band management has yet to comment on his death. Owens was 26 years old.

Rolling Stone Magazine, May 1988

CR

2006

"Not long after that, I went public."

One of Robbie's new tunes played softly in the background, and the kid, Dusty, sat uncomfortably on the floor, legs crossed, listening to all the insanity Robbie could spew. He was surprised the guy hadn't written him off as a mental case like so many others before him. He kind of wished he had.

"I've read about most of that," said Dusty, a hint of reverence in his voice. "But it was always couched as just another Robbie Hellerman tall tale. No offence. That's not what I believe."

"What *do* you believe?" Robbie asked with genuine interest.

Robbie blamed the Chaos of Noise for Clyde's death as much as he did for Son's. And he blamed himself too. While Robbie and Melissa had been taking solace in each other, they'd left Clyde to fend for himself. It was all they could do to hold their own lives together, and ultimately Robbie hadn't had anything left for his friend. Still, he refused to believe Clyde's ridiculous death was the result of the man's shortcomings. He'd have found a way to get clean, to revamp his life like Robbie had, if the Chaos of Noise hadn't drilled so deep into his psyche. Robbie knew what it felt like to face the darkness, wondering if that night you might be killed, or that you might be enough of a screw up to let the Noise win, let the whole world fall into the shitter. The difference was, Robbie hadn't spent those years facing the uncertainty alone.

A month after Clyde's death, Robbie declared war on the Noise. Reporters had been bugging him for his take on the *incident* (that's what they called it—assholes) and he'd finally given in to Spin. He wasn't sure what the reporter expected to hear from him, but over the course of two hours, he came clean about the Chaos of Noise, charging the battery, Jim, all of it. He'd hoped that opening the world's eyes to what was going on might help enlist more soldiers to their cause, but instead he was labeled eccentric by the kinder members of the press, and a publicity hungry asshole with serious mental deficiencies by the rest. He'd never made an attempt to take any of it back. He'd stood by his story and Melissa had backed him up, but he'd never heard anyone tell him they believed him. Until now.

The kid *really* wanted him to record a CD. Was that his angle?

"I believe what you've told me," Dusty said, eyes flicking away from Robbie's intense stare. "I've read the police report. Holes in walls, trashed cars. I seriously doubt you caused that damage alone."

"Demons like to fuck things up," Robbie said.

"Sounds like it."

"The thing is, I have a feeling you're just humoring me to convince me to record for you. And I've already told you, that ain't happening."

"No way. I believe it for real. Look, we do this thing your way," he said, trying to steer the conversation back to his reason for coming. "You want all acoustic? You want me to hunt up a killer band for you? Whatever you want."

"I appreciate you indulging me, kid," Robbie said, leaning back against his torn couch. "But there's nothing you're gonna say to convince me. Even if you do really believe what I'm saying, which— call me cynical—I seriously doubt."

Dusty heaved a weary sigh and pulled himself to his feet. His giant corkscrew hairdo bounced when he rose, and he fished into his inner jacket pocket. He brought his hand back out and handed Robbie a wrinkled, coffee-stained napkin with a phone number on it.

"What's this?" asked Robbie.

"I was really hoping you'd do this for the love of the music," Dusty said, nervous sweat beading on his cheeks. "He says that would get you back up to full strength quicker. But he figured you might need some convincing."

"Who figured?" asked Robbie, growing annoyed.

"Jim."

Robbie stood up, took hold of Dusty's collar and began ushering him toward the stairs. "Should have fucking known. You think I need another person giving me shit?"

"Wait," Dusty yelped, pulling free and backing away. "I'm serious. Jim's the reason I came. I mean, I wanted to record you. That's not bullshit. But Jim tipped me off on where to find you and he's pretty insistent that you make another record. The Tranquility needs you to."

"Aw, god. Are you one of *them*?"

"No! I'm a guy who really wants to record you. I told you, I believe your story. This Jim dude came to me and told me you'd want to do this record when you found out what it could mean."

"I know what it could mean," Robbie said, shoving Dusty onto the stairs. "It could mean demons on my trail all the time."

"Just read the note," Dusty said, backing slowly up the stairs, hands forming a blockade in front of him. Robbie lunged like he was going to start shoving the kid again, then cooled off a few degrees and studied the napkin in his hand.

All he'd noticed at first was the phone number. Now he flipped the napkin over and read the single sentence printed in precise block letters.

She can still be music.

Robbie looked up at the nervous record company owner. "Is this some fucking joke? Who gave this to you?"

"I told you. Jim. Said he was a Knight of Tranquility."

"How do you know he was legit?"

Dusty allowed the hint of a grin. "He figured you might ask that. Told me to tell you it's time to get some revenge on your old buddy Clement."

Robbie grew cold. He'd shared most of his story with the press, but had never told the story about the enigmatic cowboy who'd ended Son's life with a bullet. And he'd left the man's name out when telling his story to the kid.

He turned his back on Dusty, grabbed the wall phone and dialed. After three rings a familiar voice said, "Greetings, friend."

"Where the fuck are you?" asked Robbie.

03

Unsatisfaction is nothing if not resilient.

Three years after the death of founding member and rhythm guitar player, Clyde Owens, indie stalwarts Robbie Hellerman and Melissa Evans are back with the latest reinvention of your parents' least favorite, underground pop-punk nightmare band.

On their latest release, Black Fuzz, *the duo is joined by former Sham Glam guitarist, Lammy Edgar and Gary Hope, who replaced the band's original drummer, Eric "Son" Mitchell in 1987. Replete with Unsatisfaction's trademarked spooky, glistening guitar leads and endearingly off-key vocal warblings, "Black Fuzz" shows us a pair of songwriters maturing faster than they want to. When Hellerman sings "How Come All my Friends Are Dead?" in a bouncy, almost chipper tone, the listener gets the sense that this is a man walking a tightrope between musical brilliance and madness.*

Rolling Stone Magazine, January 1991

ఆ

1991

"I think Lammy's a little too into this," Melissa said. She backed up beside Robbie in the middle of Guadalupe Street as their skinny guitar player gunned down a pair of Disharmony soldiers and gave a whooping cheer. The two men hit the ground and Lammy trotted across the street, grinning. Robbie grabbed Melissa's hand and they bolted for the cover of the huge oak trees on the UT campus.

Demons popped noisily into their plane somewhere in the distance.

"Sounded like tone leeches," Robbie said. Melissa nodded her agreement. They stopped near a limestone building and backed into a corner formed by the stairwell and the wall. Lammy joined them.

"You see me drop those two?" Lammy asked, pistol dangling in his grip. "I swear one of 'em was the dude that clipped my leg the other night. Teach his ass."

"Cops will be coming now," Robbie said. "We need to clean up as many demons as we can in the next few minutes."

"They're all over the place tonight," Lammy said. "And there's more Disharmony guys than I've ever seen in one place."

"There's more of us, too," said Melissa. The night was dark, but Robbie could see pinpricks of blue light flicker in and out in the distance as members of their army scoured the campus, taking out demons.

"Can't believe you guys used to do this shit by yourselves," said Lammy, his face painted blue by the glow of Robbie's guitar neck and Melissa's baton. "And without hired guns to fend off the humans."

"I don't think you're technically a hired gun if we don't pay you," Robbie said. But Lammy was right. Even Robbie found it hard to believe it had taken them so long to figure out they stood a better chance if they came at the bad guys in numbers. In spite of themselves, Unsatisfaction had become a tremendously influential band, and the music scene they'd built in Austin had spawned a number of musicians with the talent for demon fighting. It had been Melissa's idea to enlist them to the cause, and also her idea to invite a few choice crazies like Lammy to help out once the Disharmony guys made it clear they were gunning for the group. These were street kids and musicians with no particular affinity for the light, but they were all believers in the cause.

Zip, zip. Two more demons, close by.

"Okay," said Robbie. "Let's go."

They followed him into a wide clearing, bisected by sidewalks and dotted with bushes. India Jean, the singer for a band called Dust, trotted into view, weapon glowing. She hailed them with a wave of her arm and Robbie lead his diminished group toward her. A few others had been with them at the start of the night, but Jerry Chick and a few of his crew fanned out to chase down a running band of dissonance demons and he hadn't seen them since. Hopefully, they hadn't encountered something larger.

India Jean dispatched a pair of scream demons as they rounded a building. "There are about ten more over by the stadium. Plus, a whole bunch of women in Disharmony gear. We need to gather up some guns."

"Got one right here, baby," said Lammy.

India gave him a dubious stare. "I doubt you're up to the task alone. We need to find the Red River crew."

"They're hunting the east side of campus," Melissa said. She usually knew the schedules and locations of the city's various demon fighting crews, and Robbie had taken to calling the whole gang of them Melissa's Army.

"Let's round them up then," said India. She was a lithe woman, built like a whip with long black hair. She'd only been at it a few months and had killed almost as many demons as Robbie. Her deep brown eyes held no fear, just a touch of fanaticism that made Robbie nervous. "They're gathering like they're trying to open a portal for something bigger."

"Then let's stop them before they do," Robbie said, still nursing bruises one of the giant tentacled ones had given him the week before. "Better to keep them penned than have to put them back in again."

"What's the fun in that?" asked Melissa, poking him in one of the ribs she knew to be bruised.

"You're mean," said Robbie.

The first hint of police sirens rose in the night.

"We need to do this quickly," said India.

Robbie bristled at the way India always liked to take charge, but he knew she was right. Once the first gunshot went off, it was time to leave. No one involved in the hunt wanted to answer the cops' questions about the rising "gang violence" in central Austin. And certainly no one wanted to be caught with a gun.

They crossed the campus and came to a place where the grass sloped down toward the football stadium. The Red River crew was already there, spying on the gathering of Disharmony troops. The leader of the Red River gang was a middle aged guy named Rudy who always seemed to be stifling a cough. He chewed on a lit cigarette and waved them over with a gloved hand. His crew was draped in black, and they looked like a Hollywood producer's version of a Special Forces team.

"There aren't as many now," said India, crouching behind him.

Rudy nodded. "Yep. Whole bunch of 'em disappeared into a portal and the rest took off. I count four dissonance demons, a few screamers and a handful of humans. No problem. Saw that cowboy too. The one that's always barking orders."

Anger flooded Robbie. Clement was here. He and Melissa had been hoping to run into him. "Where'd he go?"

"Into the portal with the rest."

"The cops will be here any minute," said Melissa. "Let's take these guys out and run."

Rudy hopped to Melissa's order like a good soldier. He gave orders to two guys in his crew with deer rifles and they took out the four humans at the bottom of the slope before they knew they'd been spotted. The demons with them reacted with painful howls and began climbing the slope. India and Melissa hopped the hedge and took off toward them, glowing weapons above their heads. Robbie choked up on his guitar neck and followed. Lammy began firing his pistol behind him and Robbie cursed him for being an idiot. Bullets wouldn't hurt the demons and the humans were all dead. They might have to rethink Lammy's presence on the team.

Rudy's Red River crew flooded around him, ten in all, some with the power, others just sporting guns, though God knew what they thought they were going to do once they reached the demons.

Zip. Zip. Zip.

Oh, shit.

Tone leeches burst out of the darkness, alligator-sized collections of noise that immediately stunned the gun-toters with their presence. Most were smart enough to wear ear plugs since they didn't have the power to dull the noise, but tone leeches were the granddaddies of aural assault, and within seconds most of the regular troops were on their knees.

Robbie spun and staked one of the tone leeches to the grass. He'd killed enough now that he knew exactly where to strike, and the monster evaporated with a popping sound. India and Melissa took out two more before the scream demons reached them.

Two of them jumped Robbie and he took a mental inventory of their resources as he split one in two and sent the other one hurtling back down the hill in pieces. The zipping sounds continued around them and he knew they'd been ambushed. He counted at least ten screamers, even more dissonance demons, and at least four tone leeches. Their crew numbered six individuals with the power, and around seven gun troops, most of which were writhing on the ground with their hands against their ears. Robbie saw Lammy screaming, but he was still firing his gun. Then Robbie saw the band of people he was shooting at, closing around the scene like a red-robed cult. Disharmony troops—enough to kill them all.

Frantic, Robbie searched for Melissa. She was engaged in combat with a dissonance demon. Robbie ran to her side, jabbed his weapon in the monster and yanked Melissa toward him. "We've got to get out of here! We can't fight all of these."

"No shit!" she said, spiking another tone leech that was inching toward her ankles. "How do you expect to manage that?"

He didn't. That was the problem. But the alternative was to wait until they were overcome by numbers and killed. Lammy's gun continued to fire, God love him, and a few Disharmony troops fell. Then the gun went silent and Robbie knew he'd either run out of bullets or been killed. Time to do something.

Zip. A portal opened between Robbie and Melissa. It glimmered like moonlight on the surface of a lake, and seemed impossibly serene in the middle of such chaos. He looked through it and saw Melissa on the other side, stepping back from it as it began to hum. Then a figure appeared in the shimmer, a tall man with a trench coat and a warped cowboy hat.

Robbie raised his guitar neck and took a swing, but it went right through the figure. It tumbled him off balance, and as he was regaining his feet, Clement stepped out into the corporeal world, grabbed Melissa by the shoulders and pulled her struggling back into the Chaos with him.

Zip. The portal closed.

Robbie stood frozen as all of the demons that had been surrounding them zipped away into their own portals, and the

Disharmony troops followed suit. Within seconds, only he and his injured band of hunters remained. He stared blankly at the place where the portal had opened, life leaking away from his soul. India shook him by the shoulders.

"Let's go! She's gone." India shook him again. "You don't want to end up in jail again."

Rudy's gang ran for the shadows as red and blue lights began appearing between distant buildings. India and Lammy half led, half carried Robbie away from campus and sat him down beneath an interstate overpass. The night had grown impossibly quiet, and Robbie sat stunned amid the trash and mud, smelling the approach of cold rain.

"Dude. Are you okay," asked Lammy.

Robbie looked into his eyes but didn't answer.

"Go home," he said. "Jesus, I'm sorry, man. Just go home and we'll figure this shit out tomorrow." He jogged away, and cast a guilty glance back before disappearing around the corner. India was already gone, presumably just as eager to leave as Lammy. Robbie knew he should leave too. He was still too close to where the action had gone down to be reasonably safe from being arrested. But he wasn't worried about cops any more.

That ambush hadn't been designed to kill. The only reason they'd come was to take Melissa, and they'd saved up a lot of juice to produce those portals. Why?

Robbie sat beneath the bridge for hours, pondering that question. In the end he realized it didn't matter. She was gone regardless.

As pink light peeked around the edges of the overpass, the homeless man he saw everywhere, Marco, walked up beside him, dragging a potato sack full of cans. His jeans were torn and he wore a shirt with giant puffy sleeves and a ruffled collar that might have been white years ago. Bent spectacles hung across his nose, and his fingers were heavy with rusted rings. His Chihuahua yipped twice, then sat down behind him.

Robbie stared up at him, eyes wet with tears. Marco knelt down, placed a hand on his shoulder and whispered in his ear.

"She could have been music, but now she's just noise."

Robbie began to cry in earnest, and when the tears finally stopped, the sun was high in the sky and Marco was gone.

 CB

Vacancy Records today announced plans to record the first Robbie Hellerman solo album for release next summer. Long time recluse and former front man for the infamous indie band, Unsatisfaction, this marks an unexpected return to the spotlight for one of rock and roll's most gifted talents.

Vacancy Records Press Release, November 2006

CB

2008

"I'm ready," said Robbie.

Jim sat across from him, fingers drumming against the table.

They sat together in the same diner where Jim had first spilled the beans to the original members of Unsatisfaction. Nearly twenty-five years had passed, but Robbie was pretty sure they were using the same menus. His stuck to the table when he tried to open it.

"I hope you are," said Jim. "We only get one shot at this." Jim stirred a load of sugar into his coffee, sipped it and added more. "You sure you've got the charge."

"I've been doing this long enough," said Robbie. "I know what it feels like. The CD's still hanging tight on the charts and the fans truly love it. It's not just a flavor of the week. It's a record people will be listening to for a long time. That's what you wanted from me, right? You just do your part and I'll do mine."

"I'm proud of you, Robbie," said Jim. "I wasn't sure you could do it without Melissa."

"Neither was I," said Robbie. "But I did. Let's get this whole business done with."

"Okay," said Jim. "But remember, if Clement doesn't feel your power, this won't work."

Robbie scowled. "I told you, I'm ready! I don't want to wait any more. We're getting Melissa back tonight."

Robbie stared into Jim's emotionless eyes, trying to find some humanity. He still hated the man. Especially since he'd learned the depths of his deception.

Yeah, but Jim's not the only one who lied to you. The love of your life did too. Don't forget that.

No chance of that happening.

Robbie still grew numb when he thought of his meeting with Jim at Antone's night club over a year ago. Dusty had gone with him and when they walked through the door and saw Jim, all his old resentments about Son and Clyde and his own fucked up life came bubbling back to the surface. Jim never changed, it seemed. Smiling, he offered Robbie his hand and Robbie declined.

"What the fuck does this mean?" asked Robbie, slamming the napkin and its cryptic message down against the bar. He and Dusty took stools on opposite sides of Jim, and Dusty ordered a round of beers. Robbie stared hard into Jim's eyes and the man didn't flinch.

"It's an invitation to bring Melissa back from Chaos."

Robbie hadn't expected such frankness from a shifty man like Jim and it took him a couple of seconds to compose himself. "Melissa is dead."

"No she's not," said Jim. The bartender delivered three beers and Jim turned to Dusty. "Thank you for the drinks, young man, but I need you to haunt another corner of the bar while we speak of private business. You'll get your Hellerman solo record, I've no doubt. But some secrets are not to be shared, even by those willing to believe."

Dusty gave a reluctant nod and found a table near the front of the stage where a group of teenagers were setting up their gear for an early evening set.

"I saw it," said Robbie, ignoring his beer. "Your old buddy Clement grabbed her and pulled her into Chaos."

"So he did. And she's still there. Very much alive."

"Impossible," said Robbie, trying to imagine what nearly fifteen years of life in the Chaos would do to someone. "She'd have been killed by now."

"If they'd wanted to kill her, they could have easily done so on the campus that day. Yet they took her away."

Robbie had often wondered at their reasoning, but he'd held out no hope of Melissa's rescue. "Why?"

"Because something over there thinks she's the focus of power in this particular scene. The musician with enough talent and belief to inspire the rest to rise up. They think she's the crux of the resistance."

"And why do they think that?" asked Robbie.

"Someone might have led them to believe that," said Jim, then swigged his beer.

"If you're that *someone*, you're going to lose body parts."

Jim smiled, then thought better of it. "I am that someone, but before you start choosing which parts to remove first, you should know I had a perfectly good reason to do so."

"Which was?"

"Melissa *is* the crux of the resistance."

"Bullshit!" said Robbie.

"Cocky, aren't you?" said Jim. "Are you really that full of yourself? I'll give it to you, you're extremely talented. But is it so difficult to believe that Melissa was the truly gifted member of your band? She wrote as many Unsatisfaction songs as you did. And how many times did she chime in with the perfect bridge for a song that was troubling you, or the perfect chord change. The world thought of you as the band's leader because you sang most of the songs, and you bought into all the hype. But Melissa was the band's soul and the only reason you guys were able to learn to tap the power in the first place. Maybe it's time you start giving her some credit."

Robbie's first instinct was to pull the man up from his stool and beat on him until he felt better. But instead he stared down at the bar. It wasn't so impossible to believe what Jim was saying. He'd never bothered to consider anyone else was as integral to the resistance as he was, and now he'd been relegated to sidekick. But it made sense. Melissa always led the troops, and Melissa was the one who urged them to practice their skills, to hunt even when they were stoned or drunk or battling hangovers. She had always been the driving force in their fight against the Chaos of Noise.

And Robbie had always been quick to claim credit.

Jim downed the last of his beer and snatched Robbie's untouched bottle from the bar. "She knew all along. And she embraced her role. You haven't bitten my head off yet, so I assume you believe me. If that's the case, I'll move on to the meat of the matter."

Robbie didn't protest, so Jim continued. "Melissa's capture was something she and I planned. She didn't want you to know ahead of time because you would have objected."

Robbie's stomach grew tight and he was glad he'd skipped the beer. "She went to that place on purpose?"

"Yes she did."

"We never saw you after that day by the river."

"*You* never saw me after that. But Melissa and I spoke from time to time. She came to realize that even though she didn't like me, it would be unwise to excise her only source of knowledge about the Chaos."

The revelation that Melissa had been working with Jim behind his back made Robbie unreasonably jealous. "So you convinced her it was a good idea to let Clement take her to the Noise? She trusted you, you psycho!"

"It *was* a good idea. And as long as you play your part in the plan, we'll get Melissa back in one piece. You'll need to be willing to sacrifice."

"I'll do what has to be done to get her back."

Jim grinned. "Of course you will. Otherwise I'd never have risked such a powerful talent as Melissa."

Robbie spun around on his stool to face Jim. "No more talking me in circles. You've got me here, why don't you fill in the blanks?"

"Cards on the table, as it were?" said Jim. "Okay. First you should know that Melissa can't die over there. The concept of death is peculiar to this plane of existence, and even the servants of the Noise aren't certain what happens when they kill a human over here. For all they know, the human is reincarnated into an even more powerful musician that will one day return to haunt them. Better then to trap their most powerful enemies in the Noise itself. There's no way to escape, and every second a human spends there is eternal torture."

Blood thundered against Robbie's temples and he was once again considering the joy of violence against the asshole who'd pulled them all into this. But Jim stopped him with a hard look. "Don't start getting self righteous again. Melissa knew all of this in advance and she still chose to go through with it."

"Sorry if I'm not ready to believe you had her best interests at heart."

"She is a champion," said Jim. "I do not send champions into such peril lightly."

"Just everyone else," said Robbie, snatching his beer back from Jim. He didn't really want it, but he enjoyed the irritation in Jim's eyes when he drank the whole beer in a series of gulps.

"I thought you'd cleaned up your act," said Jim.

"I have. You going to finish?"

Anger welled in Jim's eyes. "From time to time, a champion is born who can shape the very elements of Chaos into music. Not the human sounds of string vibrations, beating on drums and vocal harmonies. I'm talking about the pure unrefined noise that exists nowhere outside of the Chaos of Noise. The stuff they want to unleash on this world that would drive humanity mad within minutes.

"These champions have the ability to better...*deal* with the Noise. It's no easy task, even for them. But if one of them can ever resist the madness long enough to shape the Noise, she'll return with knowledge of a perfect song that will close the portals forever. The good guys win at last. Does that seem worth the sacrifice to you? Melissa seemed to think it did."

"So how many of these champions have tried and failed?" asked Robbie.

"All of them," said Jim, in a matter of fact tone. "But they didn't have what Melissa has."

"What's that?"

"You. I told you, there's no known way for even champions to escape when they enter the Noise. But they all go in confident they'll be able to find a way out. You're going to be Melissa's way out."

Robbie ordered a Jack and Coke before asking what the hell Jim meant by that.

"I've spent a long time convincing Clement that I'm working both sides of the fence. He's a malcontent by nature and a Tranquility traitor to boot so it wasn't a hard sell. He understands switching teams. Plus, I tipped him off on where Melissa would be so he could snatch her. He believes me. And before you get your ire up, she knew well in advance."

I sipped my drink and motioned for him to continue.

"Clement has been a bigwig in the Disharmony since he delivered Melissa to the Noise, but I have a plan that'll not only free Melissa, it'll knock Clement back down to size. If you're willing to help."

"I've already told you I'll do what I have to."

"Figuring out who's a champion and who's just an extremely talented hunter isn't an exact science. I spent a long time maneuvering events so that Clement would know Melissa was the one. And he told the Noise. Revealing that was the only way to get her in. Now I've convinced Clement that he fucked up. Melissa isn't really the key player."

"Where do I come in to this?"

"You're going to record the most amazing album of your career. A comeback album that will have the critics drooling and the fans clamoring for more."

"No pressure there," said Robbie.

"I didn't say this was easy. You'll tour, you'll make public appearances to sign your CDs, you'll soak up every drop of love the world has for your music. And when you've got the power in you like never before, I'll convince Clement it's time to make the switch."

"The switch?"

"I've been working on Clement and I've got him convinced you're the big fish. You build up a ton of power, start hunting again, and he'll really start second guessing himself. Do this thing right, and he might take you in exchange for her."

"Might? You've risked her life on *might*?"

"I've risked all our lives. There are no certainties in this war. But I know Clement. He's scared as hell that someone over there will figure out he brought them the wrong person. And he'll do what it takes to get the *right* person in exchange. You make enough noise, so to speak, and he'll find a way to bring her out. He'll deliver Melissa in exchange for you."

"What makes you think he'll let her out? If he's convinced I'm the real danger, why not just grab me too?"

"He knows you've been on your guard since losing Melissa. And you may not know it, but you still have a ton of power from your cult following. A new record will give you more. You'll be a tough guy to take down. Clement will see it as easier to trade than to risk a knock down battle that'll throw a spotlight on his mistake."

"Okay. So she comes out, I go in. Assuming I can keep my sanity for a while, how do I get out?"

"You don't," said Jim, and to his credit, he didn't shy from Robbie's stare.

"So I'll—"

"You'll be lost, yes," said Jim. "But Melissa might come back with the perfect song to end all of this."

"Honestly, I'm beyond giving a fuck about the song. But Melissa is another matter."

"You'll do it then?"

"What kind of unfeeling creature are you?"

"If it makes you feel any better, Melissa didn't know that your sacrifice would be part of this. I don't think she would have gone along with the plan if she knew. I simply convinced her I'd find a way to get her out. She doesn't know how."

"You're a snake, Jim," said Robbie. "You know that? You have your grand motives and you think that puts you above us all. But you're no better than Clement. You're content to fuck with people's lives and damn the consequences. We didn't ask for any of this."

"But you'll do it," said Jim. It wasn't a question this time. The master knew his puppets had no choice but to dance when he pulled the strings.

"If I find a way out of the Noise, I'm going to kill you."

"Fair enough," said Jim. "Now let's talk to our friend Dusty about recording that new record. He says your new songs are wonderful."

Now, eighteen months later, Robbie sat in the diner, watching Jim stir more sugar into his coffee, counting down the minutes of his life on earth.

"Okay," said Jim. "If you're sure, I'll make the call."

"Make it," said Robbie.

Jim fished a cell phone from his pocket and hit speed dial. After a few seconds he spoke again. "Clement? It's me. I've got some news you're going to like."

႘

Robbie and Jim waited on the river's north embankment, beneath the Congress Avenue bridge. The steamy August night was creeping toward the dawn and all the bat-watchers and kayakers were long gone. It was a Sunday, and the city was calm. Traffic whispered somewhere in the distance, and an occasional breath of wind shifted the trees. Robbie felt a keen sense of loneliness, as if he and Jim were the only survivors of a peaceful apocalypse. Robbie knew these were his last minutes on earth, and he tried to cherish the smell of crisp summer grass, the taste of coffee on his tongue, and the quiet lap of water as the Colorado River crept slowly past.

"You ready?" asked Jim.

Robbie didn't bother replying. Jim had been asking him the same question every few minutes for the last hour. He was ready, or he wouldn't be here. Ready to get Melissa out of that hellhole. Ready to take her place.

"He should be here any second," said Jim, tapping his watch as if it might have stopped. "Already late, actually. I wouldn't worry about it. He's never been the most punctual of—"

The air shimmered in front of them. A second later, a portal opened and Clement stepped out. He led Melissa with him, one arm around her waist, and she seemed unable to stand by herself. Robbie stepped forward but froze when Clement raised a pistol and put the barrel to Melissa's chin.

"Hang on there," he said. "Don't want the lady to choke on a bullet."

"What's wrong with her?" asked Robbie.

Melissa was naked, and her hair was long and matted, as if it hadn't been combed or cut in many years. Her body was limp, and she cast her eyes about in terror. She was disoriented, and didn't seem to understand her new surroundings.

"You can't jump right back into reality after spending that long in Chaos," said Jim. "It will take her some time to adjust."

"But she'll be fine?" Robbie's eyes burned with tears. He was torn between the joy of seeing her again and the misery of her current state.

"'Course she will," said Clement, grinning. "She ain't been mistreated." He turned his smile to Jim. "You did good. Still can't believe you convinced your *buddy* here to turn himself in."

"He wasn't thrilled to learn I switched teams," said Jim, playing his part. "But he's in love with her, and I can think of no better motivation for fools."

Clement chuckled, then gave Melissa a soft shove. She stumbled forward a few steps and Robbie caught her before she fell. She recoiled from his arms and screamed like she was unused to a kind touch. Robbie grabbed her again, helped her gently to the ground and backed away.

"It's okay, baby," he said in a soft voice. "It's Robbie. You're out of that place now, and you don't have to go back."

Melissa wouldn't look at him. She put her face in the grass and took a deep breath. Her fingers curled into the soil and she began shaking with sobs. Robbie put his arms around her, and when she didn't flinch, he squeezed her tighter and held her while she cried. Robbie put his cheek against her back and listened to her heart thump. This was his love, alive and whole. Back from the dead, or something very much like it.

"We need to finish this before the city wakes up," said Jim. He grabbed Robbie's arm and Robbie lashed out.

"Leave me the fuck alone!"

Jim kicked Robbie in the ribs hard enough that for a second, he wondered if this was some elaborate set up. Maybe Jim really was working for the Noise. Jim pulled Robbie to his feet and loosed his sword. He knocked the side of the blade against the back of Robbie's head. "Get going. She's out, now you're going in."

Robbie stared hard at Jim, then he realized it didn't really matter if Jim was playing him or not. He was going into the Noise either way. Melissa was out and that was all that mattered to him anymore. She may have a song to save the world, but even if she didn't, she'd make her own music, live her life, grow old. Jim wouldn't have organized this whole thing if he'd wanted her in the Noise, so he'd find a way to keep her out, for good or ill, and Robbie knew that once Melissa regained her wits, she was strong enough to take care of herself. He'd never understood that before, but now it was his only consolation.

"Come on, cowboy," said Robbie, stepping toward Clement. The man's gun barrel remained pointed at his chest. "You want me, you got me. Just be careful what you wish for."

"You thinking you're the one to figure out that goddamned magic song?" said Clement, smirking. "You know that's just a legend, right?"

Robbie shrugged. "Maybe, but so am I."

He stepped behind Clement, and sound waves beat a steady pulse against his chest. He turned back to see Jim draping a blanket over Melissa's bare shoulders. Clement gripped his arm and pressed the gun against his temple.

"Close the door," said Robbie. "You never know what you're going to let out."

The world shimmered in front of Robbie's eyes. Through the haze, he saw Melissa rise to her knees. Her eyes met his and he swelled with joy when he saw the recognition there. Understanding was coming back to her. Her arms shot out and she tried to climb to her feet, but Jim held her back. Her mouth formed Robbie's name, over and over, a silent scream that quickly became lost in the growing din. Chainsaws buzzed, mountains fell, nations of children screamed at once. Blood flowed warmly down Robbie's face, and the last thing he saw before the portal closed around him was Melissa, punching Jim in the face, throwing off the blanket and lunging toward him. The shimmer faded, darkness fell, and Robbie felt a grin stretch across his face.

She had *the song* in her. He could feel it in those last seconds, burning in her soul like raw salvation.

"That woman's gonna save the world," he whispered.

Then the man who'd been Robbie Hellerman became nothing but noise.

ങ

Liner notes:

The nineteen eighties saw an independent record label boom. Great labels like Sub Pop, Twin Tone, SST and countless others were born and they released some of the most vital music of the decade, and in the process, changed the way the music industry worked. They had no ties, at least initially, to the traditional behemoths of the industry, and they made it possible for regional bands to make a living as musicians without the expectation of selling a million records, and without corporate interference in the music. Some homemade flyers, a few dedicated fans, a DIY attitude and an aging Econoline van were suddenly all the things you needed to be a touring rock band. It wasn't about making cash, it was about making music. In many ways the indie rock scene of the eighties is the spiritual ancestor of the MySpace generation.

Eventually many of the regional labels were gobbled up by the big dogs, and bands that started out as indie pioneers made the jump to super stardom. The most well-known of these are R.E.M. and arguably Sonic Youth, though they're not exactly a mainstream band. Others flirted with success but never quite broke through. My favorite of these, and my favorite rock band *period*, is The Replacements.

On any given night, they were the greatest live band on the planet. Other nights, they were too drunk to stand. Their lead singer, Paul Westerberg, belongs alongside Lennon and Dylan as the greatest lyricists of the latter half of the century, and the band's mixture of seventies pop and arena rock, combined with guitar hooks rarely heard this side of The Beatles, defined the sound that would eventually be called power pop. The band was as self-deprecating as Paul's lyrics, and unfortunately, just as self-destructive.

These were guys who wanted to gather in a garage and make a lot of noise. They never expected to make money or find any degree of success. They seemed to thrive on hardship and obscurity, and as a result they managed to sabotage every break that came their way, often it seems on purpose. They never became rock stars, yet it's difficult to overstate their influence on many of the *alternative* bands that proliferated in the nineties.

Indie Gods

"Indie Gods" is about another such reluctant band, and what might happen if they suddenly had something worth taking seriously. This story owes as much a debt to comic books and Buffy as it does to rock and roll.

Recommended Listening:
The Replacements—*Let It Be*
The Replacements—*Pleased to Meet Me*
Sonic Youth—*Daydream Nation*
Sonic Youth—*E.V.O.L.*
The Violent Femmes—*Violent Femmes*
The Clash—*London Calling*

༐

About the Author

Josh Rountree plays exclusively Fender electric guitars and amps, Gibson acoustics and GHS strings. He has crowd surfed at a Pantera concert, been stared down by Marilyn Manson, won an air guitar contest at a Webb Wilder show, been summarily dismissed by Robert Plant and stepped on by Chris Layton. He's hung out behind a bar with half of L.A. Guns, seen The Muffs perform from a porch attached to a trailer in a parking lot in downtown Dallas, stalked Billy Gibbons through Best Buy and waited way too many years before *finally* seeing Paul Westerberg in concert.

He has also touched Buddy Guy on the arm.

In addition to his rock and roll exploits, he's had a number of speculative fiction stories published in a variety of excellent venues, including *Realms of Fantasy*, *Polyphony 6* and *Lone Star Stories*. For full details, visit *www.joshrountree.com*.

Acknowledgments

Thanks to the editors who were kind enough to take an interest in these stories and publish them: Deborah Layne, Eric Marin and Shawna McCarthy. You all rock!

And thanks also to the wonderful and insightful first readers who were exposed to these tales fresh off the word processor. Your input and support helped shape these into something far more than they were. Samantha Henderson, Mikal Trimm, Lon Prater, Shaun Farrell, Eric (again!) and the members of the lamentably gone Critical MS all deserve extra special thanks.

And finally, thanks to my family and friends for all the support, particularly to Kristin, Beckett and Gibson for putting up with me. I love you all.

www.ingramcontent.com/pod-product-compliance
Lightning Source LLC
Chambersburg PA
CBHW030411020726
47493CB00003B/1028